ARROWS

OF

HEAVEN

"The end of every epic is the beginning of another."

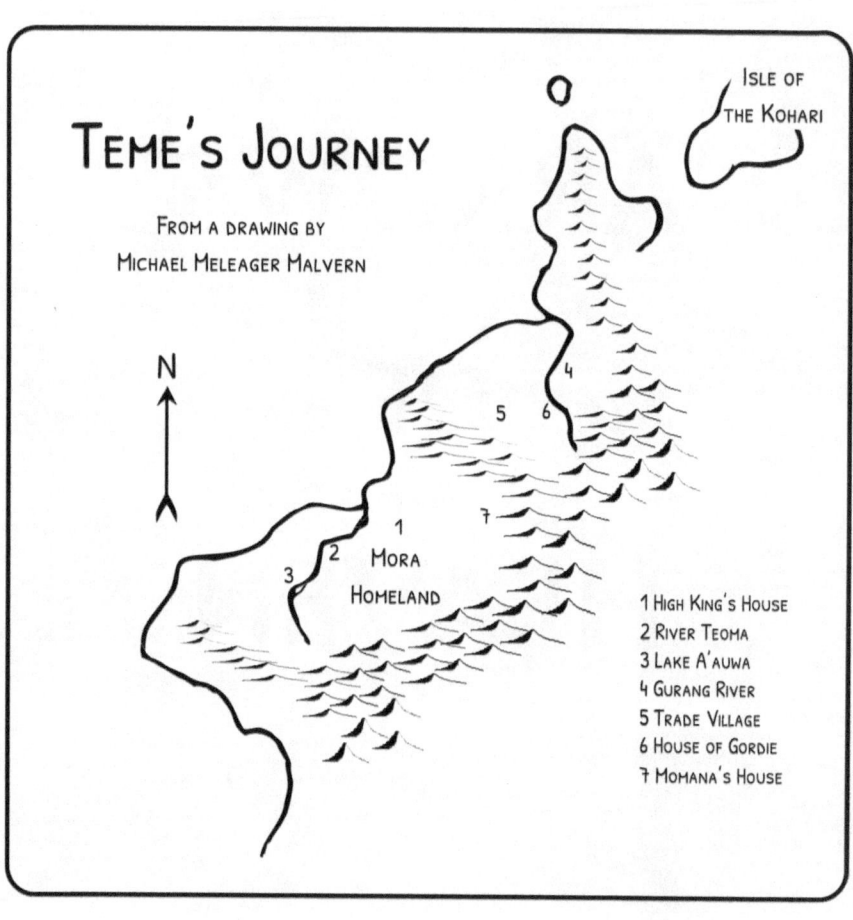

TEME'S JOURNEY

FROM A DRAWING BY
MICHAEL MELEAGER MALVERN

ISLE OF
THE KOHARI

N

MORA
HOMELAND

1 HIGH KING'S HOUSE
2 RIVER TEOMA
3 LAKE A'AUWA
4 GURANG RIVER
5 TRADE VILLAGE
6 HOUSE OF GORDIE
7 MOHANA'S HOUSE

Arrows of Heaven

Stephen Brooke

Arachis Press 2017

Arrows of Heaven
©2017 Stephen Brooke

ISBN 978-1-937745-44-8

Arachis Press
4803 Peanut Road
Graceville, FL 32440

http://arachispress.com

Part I. The Bow Bent

1. Endings and Beginnings

Over mighty peaks they journeyed,
Marareta and his comrades;
Ever they pursued the sunset!
To the land of the Diwarna,
To the land they knew as home,
Came at last the weary warriors,
Came the hero, Marareta,
There to wed the Mora maiden
Rahaita, his beloved.

I am afraid I sniffled. I remembered Rahaita. I had been there at her death. "Thank you, Ulani," I said. "That was the perfect ending, wasn't it?"

"The end of every epic is the beginning of another." There was a sadness in his smile. "But I could not bring myself to compose the one that followed."

The storyteller stared at the bamboo floor for a few seconds, before raising his eyes to me. "You are a hero of that story, Lady Teme. Someone must craft it some day."

"I was just a silly girl who thought herself a warrior."

"You saved the life of the Taona Marareta." Yes, I did, but I could not save Rahaita. At least I had avenged her slaying.

"They are lighting the torches," I noted, eager to change the subject. Ulani was unwilling.

"My apprentice should take on the task," he stated. "He might be at the house of Marareta. Did you intend to stop?"

"Toare? Isn't he still a boy?"

"A very talented boy and of an age with you, my Lady Teme." The storyteller sighed. "He will be one of the greats, as my own master, Isa. I shall never equal either of them."

That surprised me. Wasn't Ulani the favorite of my brother, the High King Poneiva? I searched his dark face.

"I will craft my mediocrities and win my accolades, but I do not delude myself that my work will last." He spread his arms to indicate all that lay about us. "Here in your brother's house I have become more politician than bard."

I knew there was truth in this. I pay attention. Well, most of the time. "Your mother says you had a gift for diplomacy before ever you came to us from the lands of the Diwarna."

"Perhaps that is one of the reasons the Lady Pua adopted me!" There was a commotion in the garden, below the open porch on which we conversed. The bard turned his attention to those who had gathered, discussing something with obvious excitement, but spoke not.

I could not be so self-contained. I stood and strained to pick up any words. "If it is important, we will learn it soon enough," said the smiling Ulani.

"But why not learn it now?" I asked him, and walked over to the top of the short, wide stairs. Ah, someone was hurrying our direction. Ulani was right, we would learn what was going on but I was not about to admit that.

Therefor, I stopped the man and heard his words before the storyteller could. Those words stunned me and I let him go on to speak to Ulani, while I stared silently out over the gardens of the High King for a minute or two, watching more lamps be lit as the skies darkened.

Ulani was seated still where I had left him, when I turned back toward the house. "It seems you will not travel alone, my lady," said he. "Many will wish to take the way to the house of Temani'itu."

"My brother?"

"I would think so. Your other brother, certainly; Lord Beka was a great friend of the old sailor."

I nodded. That was so. The two drank a great deal of beer in each other's company and told a great many lies to each other.

"My mother is already there," he continued. "It was she who sent the messengers out to spread the word of his passing. Lady Pua will always take charge, if she can."

"It is hard to lose a brother," I said. I had lost one, Maneata, years ago now. The adoption of Beka, one of those who had come to us from the sea, did not make up for it. No, even as much I loved my new brother, I missed the old one.

If ever I had a son, I intended to name him Maneata.

"Lady Pua has had many losses in recent years," said Ulani. There was no need to speak to facts we both knew.

"I had not intended to visit that house on my way," I said, "but now I shall. We must say goodbye to your uncle."

Ulani nodded and rose. "The word has surely reached Poneiva by now. Best I be there to hear what he intends. I suspect," he went on, "we will be walking at dawn."

I suspected the same. "Others, too, from all over the land of the Mora. Lord Temani'itu was loved by many."

For want of anything better to do, I trailed along behind Master Ulani as he sought my brother. Yes, there would be many journeying to the house of Temani'itu. The Taona Marareta would surely come and perhaps Toare would be with him, as he spent as much time in Marareta's house as anywhere.

After all, it had once been his father's house. I had seen Toare at times, when he visited the house of the High King with his mother. He was always mooning over Temani'itu's adopted daughter. Seeing her, whatever the circumstances, would certainly be an incentive to be there.

We would all be there; as Ulani and I had thought, we would take to our path at sunrise. So decided my brother Poneiva, High King of all the Mora.

2. He Who Sailed the Sea

I had not intended to travel this direction, but to turn on a southerly course, to walk straight across the low hills to the sacred lake A'auwa and my home. Most likely, had I traveled toward the house of Temani'itu on my own, I would have chosen to go in part by canoe for it lay close to the banks of River Teiri.

Now it would be best to take to the water there and travel down Teiri and up Teoma to my destination. In time. It was two days walk before we saw the old sailor's house. I think I could have marched it more swiftly on my own.

I was glad Revaru was not with our party, but at his own house, days away. He had been my first lover. My only lover, I should say. Many thought we would marry. At times, Revaru and I thought so, as well.

And at times we would rather murder each other. That was all over now. The young king wooed other girls, ones more willing to put up with his conceit and willfulness. It is not hidden from me that I also need find someone to put up with my own conceit and willfulness. I am in no hurry.

Were we the first to arrive? There did not seem to be anyone much about the house and grounds. Ah, there was Marareta coming to greet us. He would have traveled about the same distance as we, from the opposite direction. Probably by canoe. I realized that most other mourners would have to come further.

Being sister to the High King, I can make myself part of nearly any gathering I wish and none will object. Save my own brother, of course! Well, both of them. I now made myself one of the group that surrounded the taona.

Ulani was already doing the same. No one ever told him no, either. Oh, his young apprentice was with Marareta. I wondered if Toare's mother had come too.

"The Lady Pua has asked that I speak the rites," Marareta was explaining, as the men walked slowly toward the high house that had been Temani'itu's. I followed at a discreet distance. One sometimes forgot that the Taona Marareta was a priest. My brother had wished to name him high priest of the Mora realm but had been firmly refused. That was good as they would surely have had many disagreements.

When I was fourteen, I wanted to marry Marareta. Even a silly child like me could see he was to be a great hero. Now he noted me and beckoned. "Welcome, Teme, to the House of He Who Sailed the Sea. Come on up and walk with us." I understood the name he gave to Temani'itu's home. The great open structure in which the sailors lived below the cliffs — where the admiral lived most of the time for many years — was named the House of All Who Sail the Sea, a place where all were considered equals.

"The women are about somewhere," he said, and chuckled. "But I know you prefer to be with your fellow warriors." The boy Toare seemed to think that quite funny. At another time and place I might have shown him he was in error.

Instead I fell back a little way to walk beside him, asking politely, "Is your mother here?" I liked the Lady Mehetu.

"She is," he replied. "Panoha came too."

Her children surely remained at the House of Marareta. No, maybe not Tita. She was old enough to come say goodbye to her uncle.

Many of our party had entered the house, to find rooms and food and to ready things that needed readying, while we had walked around to the rear, into the orderly and well-maintained garden where many trees fruited and flowered. Was this how Lord Temani'itu filled his last years?

"He was not that old," someone was saying. "Somewhat less than six tens of years."

"Yet that was ten more than his brother had," I heard Poneiva reply. There was a whirring sound coming from somewhere, almost like the wings of some strange bird, a sound I barely noted as I strained to hear the speech of my brother and the others. But Toare recognized it.

"Sling!" he screamed, and leaped forward, pushing Poneiva to one side — not far, for that would take a larger man than Toare. A stone whistled by.

There was an immediate response, for most of these men were warriors. Beka and the others charged into the concealing bushes.

Toare seemed shaken. I was uncertain what to say to him but Ulani came to where we stood. "That was well done," he told the young man, his voice calm, reassuring.

"I heard slings many time when I served with King Anana. They were more common in the north." Had not his own father been slain by a sling-cast stone?

"Here is the sling," called a man. "He dropped it and ran."

Poneiva sighed. "With the many visitors and retainers here, we will never find him."

"This is not some fanatic as we have dealt with before," slowly spoke Marareta, "wishing to die a martyr. This was a warrior who very much intended to make his escape." He looked toward our little knot. "And had it not been for Toare, he might have slain you first."

"Thank you," I whispered to the boy before my brother came over to thank him more loudly.

3. The Sailor's Daughter

Who was responsible for the attempt on my brother's life? Many conjectures made the rounds of those assembled to bid a farewell to Temani'itu. Even the Lady Pua was named, but more suspected one of her cousins. Some suggested that there were still those who followed the defeated rebel cause, though none could name a leader.

Pua was too busy to take time to speak with me as more guests appeared that evening and over the next day. Va'aru was expected to arrive soon, but no other kings. Not even Revaru.

So I found myself the next morning with another who seemed at loose ends, Temani'itu's daughter, Rahiniti. "Since Pua arrived and took over, I have nothing to do!" she confided, sitting down beside me at breakfast without any other greeting. Perhaps she did so because I was a woman of a similar age. And perhaps because I, too, seemed to have nothing to do.

I barely knew the Kohari woman. No, not Kohari; once she was adopted by Temani'itu and Hihini, she was ever bit as much Mora as I. So it is with my people. She was a tiny woman, at least by our standards, and her head came no higher than my breasts. But I am taller than most.

Rahiniti spoke our language with a most atrocious accent and would fill in with words from the trade pidgin when she could not find the right one in Mora. We managed to carry on a conversation well enough, even so.

"Those are Temani'itu's wives," she whispered, nodding toward a middle-aged pair of women, one rather heavy and the other heavier.

I knew both had adult children and perhaps they were here some-where. I also knew they would have no claim on the lands and house. "Hihini named me her daughter, to please her husband, but I get along much better with Nanamiri." Which was which, Rahini-ti did not say. "Neither one has spent that much time in the house. It was up to me to run things here." She looked about. "And now it is time to leave, I think."

"You would always be welcome in the house of the High King," I told her. I was sure of that. "For that matter, my brother could make you mistress here. It is really his house, after all, to dispose of as he pleases."

She gave me a wry smile. "I think, Lady Teme, that would not be good politics. I think, too, I would not want to stay any longer."

No, I knew it was not 'good politics.' Poneiva might not care. "Then where do you go?" I asked her.

Rahiniti answered, with no hesitation, "To visit Hito, first. This I have thought on. He promised once to show me the great lake on which he dwells." She turned to me, asking as if she did not quite believe, "Is it truly larger than Aedina? I have visited there at times."

"Much larger." I was uncertain I should say what I said next. "It is where I live and where I am going. You could journey with me."

There. I had made the offer though I was not sure why. "I might," she replied, but her attention was on the gardens laid out before us. I could see tears. She had loved the old man who had made her his daughter. I had heard the story of that from Hito, who now dwelt — from time to time — at the shrine of Teva by

14

A'auwa. "I thank you," she added.

"Is the Lady Pua's husband here?" I asked her, wishing to turn our conversation some other direction.

"Naio is at sea," Rahiniti said, and picked at some melon. "Their son should be coming with Va'aru. He serves in the king's house."

That would be Mouiri. Yes, he was of the age when he would study the ways of a warrior in the house of some noble. As did Toare when he was younger. I had seen the young bard-to-be wander out onto the porch, where he now stood gazing at the buffet. Perhaps he was uncertain where to start.

He would like to sit with us, I imagined, but would be shy about it. That was up to Toare. I turned my attention back to my companion. "I wondered," I began, "did you choose your Mora name?" I hoped she did not mind my asking. Rahiniti meant 'Little Sky Woman,' more or less.

She giggled, her momentary introspection gone. "No, Temani'i-tu so named me. It was a suitable name, he claimed, as I am so small and I walked close to the sky when Hito and I crossed the mountains. He said I came down from the heavens!"

I smiled, nodding, making no comment. Once, I had heard her long Kohari name but could not remember it. Hito called her Tamba, 'Companion' in the trade pidgin, and later, Ranadi, or 'Sister,' before she was Rahiniti. I knew that they had been lovers when first she came to our land. Was she hoping to renew their relationship now? That did not seem a good idea to me!

Toare did find his way over to us. "May I join you, my ladies?" he politely and rather formally asked.

15

I pointed to a spot to Rahiniti's right. She had placed herself to my own right, which was correct in her father's house. Elsewhere, it might have been uncertain which of us should have had the higher place. Whether the girl even knew this, I was not sure; how much of Mora customs had she learned in her three years in Temani'itu's house?

The boy suddenly grinned at me. "Ma'ave has been slandering you since sunrise," he reported.

"Much longer than that!" laughed Rahiniti. "You are her rival. Her — her —" She searched for a word. "Nemesis!"

This was news to me. I barely knew Pua's only daughter, a woman four or five years older than I, married and with a family.

"I wouldn't put it past her to be involved in yesterday's incident," whispered Toare.

"I do not understand," I told them. They looked at each other knowingly.

"I am surprised Ulani has not explained this to you," spoke the young man. "One of you is likely to be mother to a future High King."

"Yes." I knew this. So what? The kings would choose whom the kings would choose.

"It is reason enough to hate you," said Rahiniti. "Across the mountains, she would no doubt have poisoned you by now."

Toare snickered. "Instead she tries to poison people against you."

"But I see now that she lies." Rahiniti seemed quite firm about this. "And of that I am glad for I do not much like Ma'ave!"

4. Feasts and Farewells

King Va'aru's party did arrive near evening — they must have hurried greatly — in several canoes. Pua's son Mouiri was with them, a tall lean boy who favored his father. Both Ma'ave and the late Ve'eta were more substantially built; perhaps Pua's other husband, the one who died defending the High King's house, had fathered them. That mattered to no one.

Also came the Lord Neatanu and his wife Hueta. As ever, people commented that the angular woman 'needed fattening.' I saw nothing wrong with her looks and sometimes suspected similar remarks were made of me. Neatanu was one of those who came from the sea with the Taona Marareta, their leader in truth, but had lived these past few years as a minor retainer, a house noble, of Va'aru — more a friend to the king than aught else.

He was also wise in the ways of the sea and had often advised Temani'itu, and Naio after him. With them, too, was Neatanu's long time attendant, Andarua. He looked very old; I had not seen him since they all came to A'auwa and the house of King Arierona nearly seven years ago.

No more nobles were expected to arrive and the funeral was to be held at sunrise on the morrow. Then there would be a great deal of talking with all these important men gathered. I might or might not be able make myself a part of some of that.

For a while, after leaving breakfast and my companions, I had watched the preparation of Temani'itu's grave mound. Workers were lining a chamber with stones where his body would lie. They were slaves, I think, but did not ask. Many captives became slaves after the civil war. They would be freed, in time; no one has been enslaved for life since the first High King ascended the dais.

Toare and Rahiniti were still gabbing when I left them. Rahiniti, mostly. Toare was learning to weigh his words, as should any story-teller, to say only what needs be said. Ulani is exceedingly good at that. All he says seems to be part of a tale he is crafting.

I did not see Ulani or anyone else interesting all day. Everyone seemed busy! No matter; I would see them all at the feast a bit later. As sister of the High King I would be expected to attend and would be seated high. To this I did not look forward, but even I have my duties.

It would be good, I decided, to talk to someone in charge about where I might sit. There was always a bit of leeway there and I defi-nitely did not wish to be beside Ma'ave! "Just below Lord Temani'i-tu's family," I was told by the minor priest who handled such pro-tocol. "The wives, the children. The youngest would be next to you. Is that satisfactory, my lady?"

Rahiniti? "Yes, that would be fine. Who will be to my left?"

His round face went blank for a moment. Figuring it out in his head, I assumed. "Ah, if there are no additions, it should be the Lady Pua."

That, too, would be fine and would put me somewhat above Ma'ave. I worried no more and napped the rest of the afternoon, awakening in time to see Va'aru's arrival.

The central room where we would gather for the late meal — no-bles only — was large, as large as that in the house of King

Arierona. There, I had feasted many times, accompanying my family who are among his vassals. It was taller, too. Arierona's house by Lake A'auwa was very old, one of the oldest in the Mora realm, and built before noblemen vied to erect the highest roofs.

Rahiniti was already seated when I allowed an attendant to direct me to my place. Temani'itu's two older daughters sat to her right and, above them, the wives. They had the highest places among the women; only a king's wife would have had precedence and none had come.

The bulky man to the right of Va'aru was surely Va'anoe, the son of Temani'itu, the only one who lived. I had never seen him before. I knew he dwelt in the kingdom of Avatu, for his mother Hihini was one of the ruler's nieces. His name was mentioned as a possible successor when old Avatu passed.

No sooner had I turned to greet Rahiniti than Pua sat down on my other side. "There will be many speeches," she warned us. "The men will try to outdo each other with their eulogies."

It was surprising that young Tita took the place to the left of Pua. But, yes, her father was the late High King Maitoa, brother to both Temani'itu and Pua. Her mother Panoha, now wife to Marareta, was just beyond her. I am not sure she should have been so high but if Pua had asked it be so, it would be so.

And beyond her was Ma'ave, looking sour. She had probably expected to sit where Tita was.

Rahiniti leaned close and whispered, "Lady Pua's son seems very interested in you."

She meant Mouiri. Ulani is not interested in any women. The

two of them sat a little below and across from us, the feast spread on its woven mats between. Yes, the boy had been eyeing me. Boys do things like that. I shrugged and helped myself to some taro paste.

"I met my other cousin's lover when I traveled with Hito," she continued. "Oorto. I liked him."

"Former lover," I had to say. "It has been long since he and Ulani parted. I have never met Oorto but I know the Taona Marareta counts him as his closest friend." The Diwarna shaman had also had a special bond with Marareta's late wife, Rahaita. For a moment, the memory of her swept all else from my mind.

I looked again toward Mouiri. A number of second cousins were arrayed below him, to his right; Pua's sisters had no living sons so some of these must be counted as his rivals in the succession to the dais of the High King. Some could also be counted as enemies of my brother and might even have had a hand in yesterday's assassination attempt.

Toare was a good way below them. His eyes also strayed in our direction from time to time, but they were on Rahiniti, not me. I did not feel it necessary to mention it to her.

Those who spoke were indeed long-winded but I paid more attention to the food than the words served at this feast. There was Marareta rising to say something. He would be concise, I knew; the taona sometimes sounded as careful with his words as Ulani.

"It was good," he was saying, "that Lord Temani'itu did have the opportunity to sail the greatest canoe ever built. We have the Lord Neatanu to thank for that, in part." He nodded in the man's direction, but I had heard that Marareta himself had first suggested the idea of the double canoe. "There are more of these now and they shall be a part of his legacy." Many drank to that. But they were willing to drink to almost anything and continued to do so long after I went to my sleeping mat.

5. Many Departures

At dawn, we gathered at the new mound behind Temani'itu's gardens and saw the old sailor laid to rest. Marareta spoke the appropriate priestly words and that was that.

I was not close but I could see Rahiniti shaking and sobbing, in front. It is the way of Kohari women, I have heard, to show their grief ostentatiously. She went away, after, with Pua and Panoha.

It was best I prepare to go away, as well. How soon could I be on my way home?

That would depend on those who might travel with me. But I did seek out the attendant who had accompanied me here and gathered all my belongings to me. That included my bow; after the attack on my brother I felt it better to travel armed.

Poneiva, however, insisted I have a bodyguard. "I will send Ruiru with you," he said. "He would like to go home to A'auwa as well." I did not know the man, but if he was born by A'auwa I understood the desire to go back.

"Who is going to live here now?" I asked, as long as I had the High King of all the Mora to myself for a moment. "Not Rahiniti, I know."

"No, not Rahiniti nor any of Temani'itu's family," came his answer. "I offered it to your uncle long ago but he had no desire to dwell here. Or maybe it was Miruhata who didn't like the idea." I could see Beka's wife advising him to turn it down. He would have left the burden of managing such an estate solely to her. "So I shall name Lord Naio as master here but, in truth, it will be Lady Pua who resides in the house."

That I knew was very good politics. None of the extended family of the late High King Maitoa, brother to Temani'itu and Pua, would have any reason to complain of their treatment. That did not mean they would not complain anyway!

Poneiva went on. "The Lady Rahiniti intends to travel with you, I hear."

"Yes, I invited her but I know not why!"

"Maybe not, but it was well done anyway," felt my brother. "Many will be going down the Teiri tomorrow and you might as well accompany them. Which way you turn when you reach the Teoma is your decision — but be sure to let me know." He might have smiled as he said this but Poneiva was quite serious. I would certainly send a message.

No doubt one or more of my fellow travelers would as well. "I think I want to go home as quickly as possible," I told him.

That was not to be. "Taona Marareta has invited us to visit his house," I was informed by Rahiniti only minutes later. "You do not mind, do you, my lady?" She seemed anxious, thinking perhaps I would abandon her.

Ah, so I would reach A'auwa a little later than I had intended. "No, of course not," I replied. It was no lie; I might enjoy a stop at the taona's house. "And name me simply Teme. You will be ready to leave in the morning?" I thought it best to ask, not knowing then how practical a woman Rahiniti was.

"I have all I own in the world gathered in a pack," she answered, "just as when I journeyed over the mountains with Hito."

I had to smile at that. "But here you can expect any noble family to give you shelter and meals along the way." It was useful to be the daughter of Lord Temani'itu. It was useful to have her as a traveling companion!

Especially as she now had the proper Mora tatoos proclaiming her a member of a high noble family. As did I, naturally. In some parts of our nation, where people were more traditional in their ways, the two of us might be regarded with a fair amount of awe.

"There will be many of us leaving," she said, as we stood on the high rear porch. Rahiniti surveyed the gardens for a moment. "I will miss all this but I could not stay here forever, could I?"

"Lady Pua would let you live here, I am sure," I said. But I understood her — Rahiniti was ready for a change.

"Oh, I should tell you she is traveling with us tomorrow. Pua intends to stay a while at the house of Marareta before returning here." She snickered softly. It was almost ladylike. "Maybe her handsome son will come along to ogle you some more."

I could play that game with her. "And Toare as well to moon over you." We both laughed and both knew the truth of what we had said. "Let's walk in the gardens," I said. "It may be long before either of us might again."

And so Rahiniti walked a last time in the gardens of her home with Lord Temani'itu, and I beside her. We spoke little.

6. Two Rivers

Va'aru and all his people were leaving, and we with them. This meant a great number of canoes traveling together down Teiri, canoes large and small. There were many marks painted onto those canoes, indicating their ownership, among them some that belonged to 'everyone' but were intended before all else for the business of the kings and high nobles. These were the craft the official couriers would use to traverse the Mora realm.

This was also the sort I chose for our travel. It was large enough for the three of us, we two women and Ruiru, and no more. We need not worry about anyone else wishing to ride with us.

We could not prevent others from floating close to us, however, and attempting to converse. Nor could we keep either Toare or Mouiri from looking our direction. The latter found it more difficult, paddling in one of Va'aru's large canoes. Toare rode with Ulani who was completely willing to move alongside us. Indeed, I think he enjoyed being an annoyance.

I hadn't known that Ulani, too, was going to the House of Marareta with his mother. All our canoes would turn north, downstream, when we reached the Teoma, but some would not continue the journey to Aedina and the House of Va'aru. Who would be staying with Marareta? I asked myself. Ulani and Pua and Toare, of course, and Rahiniti and my attendant and me. I didn't think Pua had any servants with her. Beyond that, I could only guess.

Teiri was broad and shallow. In some seasons, I had heard, one could wade across even this far down the stream. An occasional crocodile basked in the water or on the sandy banks. These were the harmless catchers of fish; none of the great man-eaters live in the rivers of our land. They would have to be able to climb the cliffs to get here! Almost all the land on either side of the river was cultivated, fields and groves lying behind the huts built near the water or, sometimes, above it on docks.

This was the richer, warmer, moister heartland of the Mora nation, more thickly peopled than the drier uplands of my own home. Those who lived here tended to be content and to care less for the old traditional ways than elsewhere. But even here, there could be unrest. I heard of such things in the house of my brother.

It should be a journey of a day and part of another day to the House of Marareta, an easy journey, carried by the flow of the rivers. Everyone pulled over to the bank shortly before we reached Teoma and there we spent the night beneath a sky of stars.

"I never saw stars so bright as in the high mountains," spoke Rahiniti, who sat beside me sharing some dried papaya. "It seemed like one could reach up and pluck them from the sky."

"Aranu has said that to me, too," I replied. "He was one who crossed them with Marareta. As did your Hito."

"Not my Hito," she corrected me. "But yes, he told me of that journey. Hito is the only man to cross the mountains three times." He might not be hers but she did sound rather proud of him.

If the tales of Marareta were true, there was one who had crossed even more than Hito — Hurasu, the wizard who ruled beyond the high peaks. But the taona claimed that he had lived thousands of years so he had plenty of time to climb wherever he wished. I wanted to believe the taona's stories but it was sometimes difficult.

Teiri joined Teoma the next morning and so did we. Haze still hung over the waters but cleared with the day; it was yet the drier of seasons in our land but that was coming to an end, as daily rains began to come in from the ocean. Even now, there was a good chance of an afternoon shower.

It was sprinkling when we arrived at the village by Marareta's house. "I have not been here since I visited with Hito," spoke Rahiniti, as we paddled to the shore. "Three years has it been, or nearly. But I have passed by since." The other canoes of King Va'aru were those that passed by now, their crews calling out farewells to us. I considered waving toward Mouiri, just to confuse the boy — but I must say I was glad to see him among those departing.

Beside us, Ulani and Toare pulled their craft ashore, and three more canoes followed us in. I was surprised to see Neatanu and his party among those who rode in them. That is, his wife and faithful attendant, plus a couple of Va'aru's warriors. Marareta's house would be crowded. Maybe we should not stay long.

So where was it? I had never been here though, as Rahiniti, I had passed by on the river. We gathered our packs — and I, my bow — and followed the crowd up a path beside a small, clear stream, overhung with fruit trees. Citron, I think they were. And there was the House of Marareta. Small, as the homes of nobles go, and said to be very old, it was set on a low hill. Many of the oldest houses were, for defense, in the days before the first High King. Arierona himself had told me that, for his house is so placed as well.

"I'll make sure you get a good sleeping chamber," promised Tita, who walked beside us. "You don't mind sharing, do you?"

Neither of us objected. I thought it likely in this fine weather that I would sleep on a porch rather than in a stuffy room. I had not had time to spend with Tita before, though I suspected she and Rahiniti knew each other well. The girl was about fifteen now, wasn't she? And large, already towering over little Rahiniti. She would look much like her Aunt Pua in time, I was sure.

Her Aunt Pua had ambitions for her. Tita's name had been suggested as a possible match for Revaru and, honestly, I thought it might not be a bad idea. But she was still too young for anyone to speak seriously of it — and this self-possessed young lady would certainly have her own opinions.

Rahiniti stopped and looked up at the building. "I last saw Hito here," she murmured. "And last — held him."

"More than held him," put in Tita, with a bit of a smirk. "But Aunt Mehetu won't mind, even if she is going to marry him!"

7. An Overcrowded House

It was not Marareta nor any of his family nor even the other guests I sought out, as soon as I had stowed my belongings away. No, I must visit Rika and Hepetea, and their children, before all else. Rika was one of those who crossed the mountains with the taona, and later became his personal attendant. Now he oversaw much of the day to day business of this house and estate.

Under the guidance of Panoha, of course, who truly ran the place. Moreover, he often was away with Marareta. Rika was also perhaps the closest friend of Hito.

"So the Kohari girl returns," remarked Hepetea. "The Lady Mehetu will have thoughts about this." One of her babies played in her lap, as we sat in their quarters on thick grass mats. The crocodile motifs woven into them spoke of Diwarna craftsmanship.

They would have insisted that I, being noble, sit separately from them, and have my own food bowls. This I prohibited at once! "Tita told me Mehetu is to marry Hito," I said.

"So it seems, though I think no pledges have been given. Toare no longer needs her full attention!" Rika smiled at this little jest of his before going on. "Hito has visited here from time to time and they renewed their, ah, close relationship."

To this, Hepetea added, "It took a while. Hito still sought his direction."

Rika nodded. "This is so. She will finally travel to A'auwa to be with him, the next time our taona goes south. At last she shall find out how a poor priest lives when he is not a guest in a noble household!" Both laughed at this. Both loved Hito, I knew.

I might have stayed with the pair — and their children — the entire time were it not my duty to be seen by my host, at least now and then. And, too, I had an obligation to Rahiniti as my traveling companion. So I went to seek out the others after a while. That meant little more than stepping out into the hallway and following it, for Hepetea and Rika dwelt in the house itself, unlike most of the servants.

"We shall all come together for a meal shortly," spoke Panoha as she passed me, hurrying somewhere. "In the gathering room."

Which was the large central room opening before me at the end of this hall. I crossed it and found my way out to the largest porch, on the southern side of the house. As is common with such porches, it opened to the gardens. Those were large and merged with the fields beyond them, filled with a great variety of fruit trees. Citrus, many, I could tell from my high vantage, but might not name what varieties without moving closer.

On a mat to my right sat Mehetu and Rahiniti, conversing as if old friends, with many smiles and laughs, and near them, Tita. The girl mostly seemed to listen. Mehetu waved me over.

"We were arguing," she informed me, almost managing to keep a straight face, "over which should have precedence as Hito's wife."

My only answer, as I took a place beside them, was, "I think, my ladies, I would wait until he actually decided to wed someone." Tita could not help snickering. I had seated myself between her and the older women though I could have claimed the highest place. It is good to be gracious about such things in another's house.

30

That does not mean I need necessarily curb my tongue. "It took him long enough, after all," I went on, "to decide to become a priest of Teva."

"We always knew he would," came Rahiniti's matter-of-fact reply. Mehetu nodded in agreement.

It was she who said, then, "I will not be going south at this time but Toare intends to travel in your company, he and Ulani. They will turn aside to visit the Taona Isa."

I glanced at Rahiniti but made no comment on this. Mehetu was certainly well aware her son had long had a crush on the girl. Ha, maybe she hoped he would distract her from Hito!

"Three generations of bards, masters and apprentices," I remarked. "That would be good to see and good to listen to."

"That it would," agreed Mehetu. All knew she loved the old tales and those who sang them. "Here come those who wandered." Others of our party were coming up the steps from the garden, the Taona Marareta among them.

"Come," he called to us. "Let's eat!"

8. Food and Drink

I might have chosen otherwise out on the porch but here at Marareta's supper I was directed to a spot to the left of Panoha, placing me higher than all the other women in the house. Panoha, of course, took precedence in her own home.

Poor Hueta had to be at the end of the row but that put her across from her husband so perhaps it was just as well. Andarua, though not considered noble, sat beyond Neatanu. No one has ever explained to me exactly how we decided which of those who came from the sea were noble and which were not.

Nothing much of importance was spoken for some time as we filled ourselves with pork and fowl, with taro and yams and fruit and anything else within reach — or that could be passed to us. There was plenty of good millet beer, though none of us drank deeply of it, save Lady Pua. She is a larger container than most and needs more filling maybe!

"Soon," spoke up Neatanu, after a sip of that fine beer, "we might have coffee to drink with our meals. Is that not so, my Lady Teme?"

I nodded but before I could answer — my mouth being too full of rich duck meat — the taona asked, "Coffee? Where did you find coffee in this land?" He looked from me to Neatanu.

Who said, "We have Andarua to thank for that," and turned his eyes to his attendant, the man who had served him for decades, I understood.

"Yes, sir," spoke Andarua. "You may remember I kept a stash of the good stuff for the Nathans and let Samuel, um, Samua you called him here, make coffee for the crew. I was planning to roast some beans, the way I usually did, when that storm upset my plans." He chuckled. "All our plans. Anyway, sir, I still had them with me when we hopped onto the lifeboats."

Neatanu took up the tale. "We decided to germinate them when we finally ended up at the big lake, see if we could grow some coffee in this country. It looked like good land for it up there." He glanced toward the old man. "We both had seen coffee grown and knew a little about it. Enough."

"Bought fresh in Panama so we figured they'd still be good, some of them," said Andarua. "You weren't in the know on any of this, being off here and there and across the mountains."

"And then we had to leave, too," Neatanu continued. "But we had already handed the project and the seedlings over to Lord Amapa and his daughter." He gave me a little bow of his head. "Bafa has kept an eye on the project but let Teme and her family tend to it."

"They grew well," I announced. Most of them.

"And they have flowered and put on berries and those berries have been planted in turn, so we have a second generation of trees going now. Soon to have berries on them, too, and at last maybe a cup of coffee!" finished Lord Neatanu.

The taona slowly nodded his head, in seeming approval. "I have missed coffee." He smiled and added, "But tea even more. It would not be surprising if tea grows wild somewhere in this world."

"We might recognize it," said Hueta, turning to her husband. "We have seen plantations."

He shrugged. "I fear that is knowledge that will die with us, my dear." To me, he said, "I shall depend on you to check on the trees when you get home, Teme. There is no one I trust more."

"And I look forward to sampling this magical drink someday," I replied — even though Bafa had warned me I would most likely hate it. I looked forward to seeing Bafa, too, and perhaps besting him once again in a match of archery.

From her place between Pua and Tita, Rahiniti suddenly asked, "Will there be time for a poem?" She could have been speaking to either Ulani or Toare, as they sat side-by-side across from her.

"One of the short ones, maybe," felt Ulani. He knew many were tired. He might have been, himself. "I should let you present something," he said to Toare.

The boy did not look enthusiastic. His long, somewhat homely face — rather like his mother's — already made him appear glum about something or the other much of the time. "If you wish," he murmured. "Our friends might prefer to hear a master."

Ulani laughed. "Isa is too far away!"

"I think we can make do with you and my son, Master Ulani," said Mehetu.

"And you are a great storyteller yourself," added Pua. She took considerable pride in her adopted son.

"But Isa is, indeed, a far greater storyteller," he said, and seemed inclined to leave it at that.

Rahiniti was not. "So what makes a great bard?"

I was inclined to say a loud voice but had the wisdom not to. Instead I said, "Practice," which was, perhaps, just as bad. I was ignored; this often happens.

"Mehetu could have been a great bard," said Ulani, with a slight inclination of his head toward the tall noblewoman.

"A woman storyteller?" Toare was skeptical, even if it was his own mother. "I've never heard of such."

"Why not?" I asked, with more belligerence than was truly needed.

"Indeed, why not? Women can do whatever they wish. There have been great women warriors," Ulani maintained. "Why, one is right here with us!"

"I know the songs of some of them," an amused Mehetu informed us. "They are not sung much anymore."

"Teach them to Toare," I told her.

"I have tried but he thinks them old-fashioned." I shot the boy a disapproving look.

Ulani was more polite but did shake his head. "Then I must set my apprentice this as his next task. But tonight, I would wish him to give us one of the old tales of love. Out on the porch, with the taona's permission."

"Granted," spoke Marareta. "Your voices are always welcome here."

I went out to listen with the others but must admit I fell asleep before Toare finished.

9. Children and Parents

"It is time you met my brother and sister," proclaimed Tita. "I am surprised neither my mother nor the taona has shown them off to you yet."

A child gripped each hand. "I held Maratoa many times when he was a baby, and still at the House of Arierona," I answered. In the days his mother was yet alive. One of his mothers. The handsome little boy looked up at me, his sea-colored eyes regarding me boldly from beneath thick, dark brows. He would be around five and he reminded me greatly of his true birth mother, the priestess Pana'a.

"I'm Whahiwi," piped up the little girl. "I'm twee!"

"Almost three," came Tita's amendment. "I know you haven't met her before."

"I greet you, Rahiri," I said. "And you, Maratoa."

"I greet you," the boy replied, very carefully. Someone had made certain he learned the proper words. Then, with a voice expressing just enough awe to be both endearing and embarrassing, he asked, "Are you a great warrior? My father said so!"

"Um —" I answered.

"She is," Tita assured him. "Toare is going to compose a wonderful epic about her!" She giggled. "Once his mother teaches him how it is properly done."

"I'm going to be a warrior, too," he stated. "Can I play in the garden?"

"All of you," spoke the Taona Marareta, approaching. "I wish to speak with the Lady Teme." Tita hustled the pair down the steps and out into the trees, as my host and I seated ourselves on the porch.

"I would not mind Ulani having a part in this conversation," the taona began. "Perhaps he will join us later." He smiled. "In the mean time, we can talk about him."

"I understand that he and Toare will travel with us, some of the way."

"Yes, and rejoin me and his mother later. We leave for the High King's house in a few days."

"Didn't my brother just see you?" I asked.

"The attempt on Poneiva's life raises new questions. We must talk." He waved to a servant. "Bring us fruit, will you? And water."

He turned his attention back to me. "I have been discussing things with the Lady Pua, of course. She is still an important fig-ure."

But not as she was once. "I know of her ambitions for Tita," I told him, "and I say she is welcome to Revaru. She might just straighten him out!"

Marareta ignored my attempted levity. "Pua may make all the plans she wishes for her niece, but Panoha is Tita's mother, and I have become her father."

"Tita will have something to say about it too."

He did see humor it that. "Yes, she will." He gave me a long look. "Pua also has ambitions for her younger son." It took me a few seconds to catch his meaning.

"Me? He's just a little boy!"

"Mouiri has ten and seven years now. Not that much younger

than you, Teme." He looked up as the servant returned and placed bowls before us. The taona picked out one the little sour oranges and went on. "You realize if anything were to happen to your brother, Teva forbid, the boy would be the foremost candidate to take the High King's dais."

"And having me as wife would give him even better odds." I knew well that if I had a son, he would also be a likely choice to rule all the Mora. How closely were Mouiri and I related, anyway? Third cousins or fourth? I'd have to figure that out sometime. Or ask my mother — she always knew who was kin to whom.

Distant enough, anyway. I had heard in the ancient times, those evil days before the first High King ruled, that high nobles might marry their own sisters! That was one of the old ways I am happy to leave to the past.

"There are others who might mount the dais of the High King, of course," he went on. "Ikataki has been striving to make himself a leader among the modernizers."

I knew the man, a second cousin of Mouiri and the late Ve'eta. "He is no Hareata," I sniffed.

"Nor even a Pua," he agreed. "But many of his faction think your brother is too traditional."

I looked closely at the Taona Marareta. "Do you?" I asked him.

"Poneiva prizes moderation. So do I."

"Then you are neither a Parrot nor an Owl," I said, grinning. That was what the two parties had taken to calling themselves — originally meant to insult each other but now names worn proudly.

He laughed. "But I seem to flock with the Parrots!" Then, as quickly, he sobered and said, "The question is which bird sent a stone toward your brother."

"Couldn't there still be rebels?"

"It is possible that the extreme traditionalists, those who would have no High King at all, were responsible. No one really believes that." He shook his head and picked through the bowl of fruit again for a few seconds before speaking on. "The tensions that led to civil war still exist and there are many restless people who still support those who call for the ancient ways and taboos. I know you understand these things, Teme, though some would see only another young noblewoman when they look at you, someone without a serious thought in her head.

"Hareata and Temani'itu are gone, Pua is no longer the force she was, but you are here." He peeled another orange and spoke no more.

10. Against the Current

The taona was right. I did pay attention to what went on around my brother. Politics had long been part of my life and Marareta himself was largely responsible for that. Would Poneiva now be High King had not the Hero from the Sea come to the Mora?

Not that my big brother would not have been a great man anyway!

It was true that many of those who once led the 'Parrots,' those who favored the newer ways, were gone or had lost influence. Va'aru was still an important voice, and Va'anoe was firmly with him. The son of Temani'itu was respected and might well succeed King Avatu, but he was not a forceful leader.

Rahiniti interrupted my reverie by sitting down beside me. She was Va'anoe's sister now, wasn't she? I hadn't really thought of that before; in theory, having been adopted by Hihini, her son would be among those eligible for the dais of Avatu someday. But none would actually consider that seriously.

"Will we take the same canoe as before?" she asked me.

"We might as well." Rahiniti had only asked to have something to say. "Ulani and Toare will have their own."

She sat quietly for a minute or more. "Even though I have made great journeys and had great adventures, I am nervous."

To see Hito again? No, not that — or not just that. "You are starting all over again," I observed.

"Yes. I have only a name now. No wealth, no home."

"That name can carry you far," I told her. "At least as far as a husband."

"And then I might have wealth and a home. Perhaps that would be enough." She sat there, her chin resting on her knees, for a moment before turning to me. "Not enough for you, Teme."

"Maybe it should be," was all I could answer.

"Marry Toare," she said, not sounding at all serious about it. "Then he would no longer pester me!"

"One could do worse," I admitted. I rose and my companion rose beside me. What a pair we made! I a head-and-a-half taller than the compact Rahiniti, lean where she had the rounded muscles of a dancer. "Do you still dance?" I asked her.

"I go through the movements we learned in the temple each morning when I rise," she answered. "But, no, I do not really dance."

"You must learn to dance as we Mora do. There are many in the House of Arierona who could teach you."

"I would want a man as my instructor," she said. "Kohari men do not dance."

So I had heard. "I am going to say goodbye to my friends Rika and Hepetea. Would you wish to come?" She looked uncertain so I added, "They have children." I knew Rahiniti could not resist that. Hito had told me things.

We gathered that night for our last meal in the House of Marareta, on the porch. It was pleasant there and the evening just cool enough, following a light afternoon rain. After, Ulani gave us a longer epic, but it was not his tale of Marareta's journey over the mountains. I think we had all heard that one enough times. Especially Marareta!

And in the gray dawn, we walked down the path to the river, to be on our way. I saw a small canoe with a single paddler draw away from the shore as we approached.

"That is the messenger I send to your brother, telling him you have departed," said the taona, who had walked with us. "In two days, I myself shall set out for his house."

No other of his household had accompanied us to the banks of Teoma, not even Toare's mother. He and Ulani silently stowed their packs in their canoe. We would lose the company of the story-tellers when they turned aside to the home of Isa. Above the joining of Teiri that was, but I was not sure how far.

Ruiru and Rahiniti were already pushing our canoe out onto the water. I had best join them. "I give you my farewell, Taona," I said.

"And mine to you, Lady Teme. Be sure to give my greetings to all at A'auwa. They, too, I shall see before long."

I hurried down to the sandy shore, my pack in one hand, my bow in the other, and climbed into our craft where it barely floated in shin-deep water. "The current will be against us now," remarked Ruiru. "It will not be so easy as it was coming here!"

"Oh, just leave the paddling to us," I told him.

"Better yet," spoke Rahiniti, "toss a rope to our fellow travelers and let them tow us!"

That would not have worked well, for our canoes went side-by-side most of that day. This was the doing of the bards, for both liked to gossip as they went. I would as soon have paddled in silence and enjoyed watching the shores we passed. This part of the river, and that which lay beyond us, was not so familiar to me, for I had mostly traveled overland between the House of Arierona and that of the High King.

We passed Teiri late in the afternoon. Canoes large and small were coming and going on both rivers. Many were piled with trade goods, perhaps from the kingdoms to the north, perhaps all the way from Diwarna lands. I had always intended to travel across the hills someday and visit there. I still did.

To our right, a little later, appeared one of those places on the riverside where travelers might rest. These were set aside by the orders of the kings, in part for the use of couriers, but also for those who traded up and down the waterways of the Mora lands.

It was not yet late but we might not reach another before dark. Not that we would be prohibited from pulling over anywhere to sleep, should we wish. "Let us stop here," I called.

11. In the Dark

Three others arrived with the dusk, coming in two canoes, one a few minutes after the other. One, I could see, was an official messenger; the others, man and woman traveling together, might have been traders. I was too tired to do more than give a greeting and turn to our meal of dried fish and fruit.

An open hut provided shelter to all who wished it but on this night, with a clearing sky, there was no need. Rahiniti fell asleep immediately. In some distant world, it seemed, I could hear the low voices of Ulani and Toare, still finding things to talk about, until I, too, slumbered.

They were silent when I roused from sleep some time later. Ruiru seemed to be awake; he lifted his head and looked toward the river, then lowered it and resumed sleep. Ah, another canoe had come ashore. Three or four figures were getting out, more travelers.

I lay listening to the stars, unable to quickly fall asleep again. My sore muscles might have had something to do with that. I massaged one shoulder and then the other.

I heard a whisper. "Which one?"

"I don't know," came a low reply. "I wasn't told there would be two."

"If we had any light we could read their tattoos," came the first voice again.

A third voice entered the conversation. "Grab them both and let's get out of here." I could see figures, dark silhouettes against the sky, standing almost over me.

"What is this?" called out a gruff voice to my left. Ruiru had apparently not fallen fast asleep yet. I took the opportunity of the unexpected distraction to roll over and away from the intruders. I saw one grab for Rahiniti where she slept, still oblivious, and clasp a hand over her mouth.

A weapon! I had nothing on me, not even a knife. It was too close for my bow, I knew, even as my hand found it. But unlike Rahiniti, I had the use of my voice. I shouted out a good Mora war cry as loudly as I might. Even Poneiva would have had difficulty matching me.

Ruiru was on his feet. I could see the glitter of a flint knife in his hand, the only weapon he had on him. Voices arose beyond us in the dark — I had surely awakened everyone in the camp.

The strangers — I could clearly see now they were four in number — held knives of their own. They must have realized the foolishness of attempting battle at this time so they backed away, the struggling Rahiniti in the arms of one. Her mouth was covered no longer and she was nearly as loud as I!

Ulani and Toare rushed toward us, and the courier not far behind them. "Forget the woman," called one of the would-be kidnappers. The captive released, all four ran for their canoe, rapidly launching it onto the dark river. One, almost, was left behind, splashing through the water beside the craft before he made it on board.

By then, I had my bow in hand and an arrow nocked. A farewell shaft followed them into the night. I was sure I hit one. Perhaps even the one for whom I aimed.

When it was ascertained that no one was harmed, we all settled down. Rahiniti was surprisingly calm about the whole thing, brushing off the sand from being thrown onto the ground, and re-joining us. The trader couple returned to their sleeping mats, having no part in any of this, while the rest of us held council.

"Why would they want Rahiniti?" asked Toare.

"I am not sure they did," I had to reply. "They seemed only to know they were to kidnap a woman."

Ulani considered this information. "So they might have been after you. The sister of the High King would be a greater prize." He gave a little bow toward Rahiniti. "No offense intended to you, my lady."

"But it could have been either," his apprentice pointed out. We all had to admit the truth of this.

"You must return to the House of Marareta," stated Ruiru. "It is not safe to travel."

"Or better yet, to your brother's house," Ulani said. I made no answer to this, nor did Rahiniti.

What I said was, "They hoped to do this quietly and escape before anyone was aroused. They might not have even known the two of you were with us." This I addressed to Ulani and Toare.

"They certainly did not expect much resistance," Ulani agreed. He turned to the courier. "You know who these women are?"

"I do, my lord," he replied. Ulani would normally not have wished to be addressed so — even if he was, technically, noble — but paid it no heed now.

"Then you know news of this should travel at once to the High

King. I depend on you to attend to it."

"A messenger should travel to the Taona Marareta's house as well," added Ruiru.

The man gave a respectful nod, saying, "It will be done," and with no further words went to his canoe and disappeared onto the night-hidden Teoma.

"So, we know not which of you was to be kidnapped," Ulani said. "Nor the reason why. We shall head downriver at dawn and let others sort it out."

"Then you will head downriver on your own," I replied. There had been time to think.

Rahiniti backed me up at once. "We go to A'auwa."

"And we are the only two whose votes matter on this," I told him.

I could see a slight smirk on Toare's face, even in the darkness. Ulani only sighed.

12. Two Canoes

"It is decided," spoke Toare, in his most professional voice. "I shall not turn aside to Master Isa's but accompany you all the way to A'auwa."

I did not mind that the bards had made this decision. It might be good to have another warrior along with us. Unlike Ulani, Toare had been thoroughly trained in weapons.

But I had to point out, "It will be crowded in our canoe."

"I can sit in his lap," suggested Rahiniti. I did not laugh when he blushed, though it was difficult.

"You will take to walking soon after," said Ulani. "The stream on which Isa dwells is not far below the first falls." He seemed to think on something for a moment. "You could stop there at the master's house for a night or two if you wish. I shall stay no longer than that before I journey back to Poneiva."

"It would be safer to travel on quickly as possible," was Ruiru's opinion. I thought he was right.

As did Ulani. "Probably so. I shall have to bring beautiful women to Isa some other day."

Through that day and the day after we paddled south against the stream of the Teoma. It was not so strong at that season, just at the start of the rains. I have heard progress is nearly impossible when Teoma is at full flood.

The countryside about us was still rich but had been slowly rising. More of the old wild forest grew here, tall trees that had sprung from the earth before ever the Mora set foot in this land.

There was forest like that on the shores of A'auwa.

I felt a bit homesick, seeing them.

And more days we traveled and more nights we slept beside the river. It was decided — apparently by Ruiru — that we would not use the sites intended for this but camp at randomly chosen spots, so none could predict our location. I think my brother did well when he chose our bodyguard.

The man looked very ordinary, neither particularly tall nor short, heavy nor lean. I thought he served as second to some noble commander, as high as a commoner might rise, normally. So was Hito once. I chose not to ask him of this.

On we paddled. The land to our right, the west, was generally drier, while many little streams joined Teoma on our left, carrying water from all the wide lands between us and the great mountains. At last, Ulani pointed out one of these streams and we pulled over to the bank at its mouth.

"Here we part," was all he said, as Toare clambered out of one canoe with his gear and fitted himself into another. We watched the storyteller paddle up the placid tree-shadowed little river for a while, taking the opportunity to rest before launching once more onto Teoma.

"It is most beautiful at the House of Isa," said Toare, as we stroked upstream. "A good place to rest but I would get bored, I think."

"What?" I asked. "Would you not spend your days composing masterpieces for us?"

"Isa only does that between dawn and noon," came his reply.

"After that he drinks."

Rahiniti nodded wisely. "It is good he does not do it the other way around."

Ruiru said little as we went on but I think we amused him. We were children, truly, beside the veteran. Oh, certainly he wasn't quite old enough to be father to any of us — more like an older brother.

Yes, Toare and I were children, both of us just past two tens in years. Rahiniti was surely a little older, but not much. Hito was uncertain of her exact age; she might have been uncertain herself.

"Do any of you know how much further we must paddle?" asked Ruiru one evening. "I have never been this way."

The truth was that none of us was sure. "I've been on this part of the river but once," I admitted. "And we were going the other direction."

Toare was only slightly more knowledgeable. "I have traveled a round trip with Ulani. I think it should not be much further to the falls."

Whether 'much further' meant a day or a week, he could not say. Fortunately, it was a day. We heard the music of the rushing water early the next afternoon and soon pulled into a broad, shallow, and rock-riddled area of river below the falls.

They were not high, those falls. "In the full rainy season these are more like rapids," stated Toare. Whether he had seen them at that time or only heard this he did not say. I did not care and I had heard the same. Many canoes were on the banks here, as this was a place where most took to the road. Or left it. It was possible to navigate Teoma for a short distance above the falls; most, however, felt it was impractical and the river there was used mostly by those who lived along it.

There was also a small village and a barracks. Arierona kept warriors stationed here, near the northern border of his realm. "I must speak to the commander here," announced Ruiru, leaping ashore as we brought our canoe to the pebbly bank. We did not see him again for a while.

13. By the Falls

A man was hurrying southward from the hut of Arierona's warriors, taking the road toward A'auwa. A courier was my guess, sent to tell of our coming.

Ruiru's doing, of course. I turned my attention back to my friends. Friends? I have not called them this before but they were. Even Rahiniti whom I had not known long.

Toare and I had been friendly for years but maybe not friends until now. We hadn't seen each other often enough for that. He was a good boy. I was almost willing to wish him success with Rahiniti.

The three of us stood regarding the falls, silently. Often had I visited the high falls that lay above these, the Falls of Pana'a, where Lake A'auwa rushed down to the Teoma. There was surely a name for these falls but I knew it not.

"I like it here," Rahiniti was saying.

"You'll like it better at my home," I told her. "Maybe not *my* home, exactly. My parents' estate lies well beyond the House of Arierona and the land there is mostly rolling hills with fewer trees."

"But you are close to the mountains, are you not?" asked Toare.

I nodded. "I have seen enough mountains," was what Rahiniti had to say about that. "This place is good. Not too steep and not too flat."

Ruiru chose that moment to rejoin us, accompanied by a squat warrior. I recognized him, an officer of Arierona. As many of those who serve noble and king, he was not born in the land where he found his position.

The man was a noble so our Ruiru deferred to him, allowing the officer to say what he would. "My ladies, I welcome you." We acknowledged him with polite nods. That was safe, especially when one is a high noble and can get away with about anything. "Your attendant has asked that we provide an escort for you. There was an attack, I understand?"

I did not like his condescending tone, nor his reference to the warrior Ruiru as an 'attendant.' Even if he was one, strictly speaking. "What is there to understand?" I asked, as haughtily as I was able — and that is pretty haughty. "We were attacked. So it is."

"Yes, yes, of course Lady Teme. I shall certainly send two —" He glanced at the scowling Ruiru from the corner of his eye. "Er, four men along with you."

"It is well," I replied and turned away from him in dismissal. "Ruiru," I said, "will you see to the details?"

"Most certainly, my lady," he replied, doing his best not to let a grin split his broad face. Both went aside, to 'see to the details,' I assumed.

"It is good to be sister to the High King," remarked Toare. To Rahiniti he said, "You can take lessons from Teme."

"I would need to be a foot taller for them to do any good," she felt. The woman turned toward the water. "Is it permitted to bathe?"

As far as I knew. "It is just the river, the same as before," I told her. "When we get close to A'auwa, you may bathe in the sacred pool below the high falls. It is customary for brides to do so before their weddings." I thought on that for a moment. There might be such a visit for me someday. "But permitted for anyone."

Rahiniti splashed in the shallow water for a few minutes while we waited. It was not unexpected that some of the warriors felt a need to keep an eye on her.

It was nearing dusk when Ruiru returned to us. "We leave in the morning, my ladies," he informed us. The two of us who were ladies, that is. Toare did not count for much in his eyes, I am afraid. "Do you wish to sleep in a hut?"

The weather looked good so I shook my head. "How long are you going to stay with us?" I asked him. "Will you go back to my brother when we reach the House of Arierona?" I recalled that he was a native of our kingdom, and might well wish to remain a while.

"The High King said only to accompany you. He did not say how long." He shrugged. "I think it is up to you when I am to be dismissed, Lady Teme."

I turned to the others. "Shall we keep Ruiru?" I asked.

"Fine with me," came Toare's nonchalant reply. I knew he meant he would like the man to stay but didn't want to seem eager about it.

Rahiniti thought differently about it, thought in a way a noble might not be inclined to. "Do you have someone to return to in the north, Ruiru?" she asked. "We shouldn't keep you from them."

"No, my lady. I have no one."

"Ah, then you have us," I informed him. "Whether you want us or not!"

As darkness fell, I could not keep from thinking we were being watched. But there were many there, warriors, traders, those who lived nearby. Who could say whether a spy might be among them? Who could know if one of those who tried to take Rahiniti — or me — might sit on a mat at the next campfire?

What I did know was that we were safe here and now. I fell asleep to the dreams of the falling water.

14. On the Path

Four men, men I had seen serving the House of Arierona. I knew there were other men from other houses just as capable but it made me feel safer than might have any other escort. We took to our path at dawn, walking the much-traveled earthen road that paralleled Teoma. Here we could see the river to our left, here we could not, as our way rose and fell, turned into the countryside and then back toward the water.

It was days yet to A'auwa, I knew, but that seemed nothing now. This was my home. I recognized men and women we passed; not all nor even many, but some.

Even the trees looked like old friends. The way was steadily rising. In some places it was nearly imperceptible; indeed, in some it seemed we descended, for the country was rolling. Deep ravines opened up in places beside our pathway, filled with dark tangled jungle. At times we climbed steeply. All this would lead to the rim of the upper Teoma valley, where lay A'auwa and the wide prosperous kingdom of Arierona.

We must camp before we reached that border and beheld the sacred lake.

"This is almost as bad as climbing mountains," complained Rahiniti, as she dropped her pack and then herself to the ground. "Hito's lake had better be worth it."

"What of Hito himself?" I asked. That was as much for Toare's sake as hers. Yes, yes, it was not nice of me.

The answer was surprisingly honest. "I do not know."

"Then perhaps I should find someone else for you," I declared, not being very serious about it. "Our Ruiru is better than most, I would say."

Toare stifled a snicker but Rahiniti looked up at me and smiled rather sweetly. "Ruiru does not care for women. Could you not tell?"

I looked from one to the other. Apparently they were wiser than I in such matters. "Well, then," I laughed, "we must consider him for Ulani!"

Toare became rather pensive. "My master has had no one for all the time I have been with him. Not since he and Oorto parted."

That surprised me, though I have to admit I had never heard any mention of lovers. "Five years? Maybe we truly do need to get him and Ruiru together. Or him and anybody."

But that was no concern right then. "I'm hungry," I complained. "And I am sick of dried fish." I dropped to the ground between the two.

"We expect you to arrange feasts when we arrive," Toare told me. "Great mountains of pork and duck and chicken and no fish at all!"

"What of dog?" asked Rahiniti. "I have heard you Mora eat dogs."

"Not I," proclaimed Toare. "It's uncivilized. Why — why it's almost as bad as eating men!"

"Which it is whispered some of our ancestors did." I shivered at the thought. "I think maybe I like fish after all," I said and took a bite of mine. No, I still didn't like it.

As far as dogs went, that was something some commoners in

some places consumed. I had never seen them at a nobleman's meal. Except live ones, begging for scraps.

My eyes went to a pair of men huddled nearby. Travelers, though I had not noticed which direction they were headed. What I did notice was that one had a bandaged shoulder. Many things could be the cause of that, it is true. An arrow is one of them.

It would be a good idea to mention them to Ruiru. The morning would be soon enough. I was tired now.

But not necessarily sleepy. I sat quietly by our little fire for some time, listening to the snap of the burning wood, the sounds of the insects and frogs and night-birds. Rahiniti sat beside me, also silent, while the men snored on their mats.

Rahiniti leaned in, nearly whispering, "Ulani is not the only one who has remained alone. There has been no one for me in the three years since Hito and I were together." She shrugged and even managed a sort of giggle. "But I was very busy being a daughter and learning your ways."

I had nothing useful to say to that, I feared, though I tried. "You have begun a new life. You said so yourself." Or something like that.

"This is true. Hito belongs to an even older life. I do not know if he fits in this one." She yawned. "We find out soon, don't we?" With that she lay herself down and was soon asleep.

I stared long into the fire. I was really no different, was I? Oh, it had not been so long since I and Revaru had our final fight but I too had not known love since. Maybe I needed a new life also. And a good night's sleep.

When morning came, the two men who caught my attention were gone. I forgot about them, picked up my pack, and walked on toward A'auwa.

15. The Pool of the Moon

"It is Bafa!" I told my friends. He must have headed this way to meet us as soon as the courier arrived.

"Bafa?" asked Rahiniti. "He is a great hero, is he not?" She gave him another look as he and a pair of warriors approached. "He doesn't look it."

He did not. Bafa was a slender man of ordinary height. But I had always thought him very handsome. "He is the third-best archer in the world," I proclaimed.

"And you are the best, Teme?" asked Toare.

"Oh, no, that would be Amirea. I am second-best! But it was he who taught me to shoot with the bow."

This was not something I would tell either of them, but after my fourteen-year-old infatuation with Marareta came a fifteen-year-old infatuation with Bafa. It was certainly more serious and lasted longer.

I may have even felt a twinge of that old infatuation when he embraced me in greeting.

He turned from me to my companions. "Toare. It has been long." I think the boy was surprised Bafa remembered him. "And why are you traveling with one of the goddesses?"

Oh, Bafa. "This is the Lady Rahiniti," I told him. There was little doubt that the courier had given him this information.

"Welcome all," he said. He peered at Ruiru. "I know you, I think."

"Yes, Lord Bafa. We fished together, long ago." When Bafa first came to us, he spent much time fishing on A'auwa and avoiding responsibility.

"Long ago, indeed! You are welcome as well." As Arierona's adopted son, he could welcome anyone and was inclined to do so. "Are we ready to go on?" he asked, looking at no one in particular though I was clearly the one expected to speak for us.

"We are," I told him. "Is it far yet to Pana'a?"

"Not very." He turned toward the south. "You can see the rise easily from here."

Yes, I could see the steepening of the way, low rocky cliffs glimpsed through the forest here and there, not far ahead. We could turn aside to the falls before reaching it. If my fellow journeyers were not too tired. "Would you still care to see Maravetu, the Pool of the Moon?" I asked them. Rahiniti, mostly, I asked.

But Toare answered first. "I have always wished to."

"Why not?" was Rahiniti's reply.

"It is best if most of you men stay up on the road when we go down to the Pool of the Moon," I said to Bafa as we continued on our way. "Have you yet found a bride to swim there?"

"No, Teme. My father keeps suggesting wives to me." He did not seem to want to talk about that.

The way had already risen toward the valley rim when we reached the place of turning aside. I looked down into the ravine below the Falls of Pana'a; their roar was but a murmur at this distance. "Brides swim by moonlight," I said. "It shouldn't matter to us that it is day. You are coming down with us, Toare?" He nodded.

"You are still my responsibility, so I must accompany you," stated Ruiru. His voice made it clear that he would yield to no argument.

"We shall remain up here, then," Bafa told us. "Take not overly long, if you will. The king awaits you." He and the warriors sat down by the road; a couple stretched out to nap.

Down a steep narrow winding path through the woods we passed. Pana'a became more visible, as well as louder. It was a high falls, the highest I know, cascading through a notch in the cliff, the water plummeting to the deep shaded pool beneath — the Pool of the Moon.

I heard voices. Others were swimming. "It is beautiful," said Rahiniti gazing upward. "So beautiful — oh, I must leave it to our poet to describe!"

"I'll try my best," promised Toare. It seemed he was taken with the scene as well. He stared down at the pool. "Are you sure it is alright for men to bathe here?"

I pointed to a boy splashing in the water. "Very well then," he said, dropped his loincloth, and dove in. I was behind him a moment later. Oh, it was colder than I had expected!

I turned to where Rahiniti still stood above us, a dismayed expression on her face. What was bothering her?

Toare figured it out. "She does not wish to be naked in front of men," he whispered. "We forget she is not Mora born."

We watched Ruiru come up and whisper something to her. Rahiniti nodded and then slipped into the water, still wrapped in her loincloth. She paddled over to us but avoided looking at Toare. "Ruiru said it was permissible to swim so," she said, sounding somewhat uncertain about it.

"Of course it is," I told her. "But I do not understand why you would wish it." It probably sounded like criticism.

Toare smoothed things for me. "It is not necessary to understand, Teme. Only to let Rahiniti be Rahiniti."

I swear by Rai himself, that boy was becoming as much of a politician as Ulani. We swam not long for, after all, Arierona expected us. I let Toare get out first and slip his loincloth on while Rahiniti directed her eyes elsewhere. Those eyes looked up at Pana'a much. The fall seems unbelievably high and I thought of all the waters of A'auwa pressing behind. What if they all fell down upon me at once!

Someday they might, Bafa claims, and much of the lake will run away down Teoma. I pray to the goddess of the pool, Marahina, the Moon Woman, it will not be in my lifetime. We pulled ourselves out after Toare and prepared to climb back up to the road. Rahiniti was very soggy!

No matter. Her loincloth would dry quickly enough as we walked. Partway up the path, to one side, was a little shrine with a stone statue of the Moon Woman, no taller than my waist. A group of men sat there, heads bowed, seemingly in prayer. But one had a bandage on his shoulder. "It is the kidnappers," I cried and then let out as loud a shriek as I might to alert those above us.

This time there was no mistaking their intention. All four leaped to their feet and toward — me!

That Toare and Ruiru also leaped to get between us — Toare despite being unarmed — was no surprise. That Rahiniti did as well, was. These assailants wanted only to grab me and escape — engaging in a fight would not help anything, so they attempted to muscle past my protectors and lay their hands on me. Recognizing this, the best thing possible for all of us was for me to run swiftly the other direction, even though every part of me wanted to stand and fight.

Still, one man was able to grab my arm before I was completely free. Only one man; that might not have mattered with another woman but I am Teme! Sister of the High King! Slayer of Hara'a!

Oh, very well, I am just being dramatic and should leave that for whoever composes my epic. But I am still tall and strong and know something of fighting. Enough that he couldn't just take hold of me and drag me away. And by then, warriors were running down from the road. I wonder if the kidnappers even realized they were up there. On thinking about it, I am pretty sure they didn't know about Bafa and his two, at least.

They might not have acted if they had. The one wrestling with me saw the hopelessness of facing those onrushing warriors and turned and ran. The other three now had knives in hand — they had not drawn them when trying to grasp at me — and stood facing my friends. I saw blood on more than one body but knew not whose it was. Ruiru lunged in at one, his flint blade flashing in the mottled sunlight that broke through the trees. The man backed away, stumbled, and toppled down the long slope toward the pool. The other two turned and followed their already-flown comrade into the forest. It would be hard to track them there, especially with only a handful of men.

Bafa had reached us. "If he hasn't broken his neck," I told him, "you should be able to fish a prisoner out of the Pool of the Moon."

Part II. The Arrow Nocked

16. The Sacred Lake

It turned out the man who fell into the pool broke only an arm and a collar bone. I was not concerned for his well-being. The gash across Toare's chest seemed of much greater importance.

It proved neither deep nor dangerous. "I picked up a fallen branch and defended myself," he reported. Then he chuckled. "And so did Rahiniti, even if she had no idea how!"

The captive trudged along, his arm dangling. That he was in pain I have no doubt but it was not so far to the House of Arierona. He could bear it. From the man's few tattoos it could be seen he was not noble. Nothing about him proclaimed anything more.

Up the steep way past the cliffs we went. The road was well laid out, long used, so it was not difficult but a bit roundabout, veering to the west before turning back again. Then we stood on a broad rocky height and looked out over A'auwa, the Sacred Lake.

"It will be dark before we reach the House of Arierona," someone grumbled. I did not care. To look upon A'auwa at sunset is a wondrous thing.

"Ah," said Rahiniti. "It *is* bigger than Aedina." She attempted to peer up its length, across the dazzling windblown surface. "Hito lives on the other side?"

"Sometimes," I replied. "He might be with Arierona when we arrive."

She considered this. "I hope not. It would be too soon."

It would. We needed time to settle in and rest. And we would do so before all the light left the sky.

But many lights burnt in the House of Arierona when we approached, the lamps burning on the porches, the torches in the gardens and by the lake shore. So I remembered the house; there had been great joy and great sorrow here. I wondered how Marareta could bear to visit it at all.

It was from those weathered steps before the house I had descended to speed a shaft toward King Hara'a, poised to end the taona's life as he lay before him, the thrust of his spear stopped at the last moment. And from them I had watched the king slay Rahaita in his madness.

Best not think of that day but leave it to the bards. There were happy memories, too, of this house, of my brothers and their wives, and the many children who played here. Once, I was one.

Arierona sat on a mat before his entry, waiting for his guests. He honored us greatly by this. We ranged ourselves in an arc, there before the king on his porch, travelers, warriors, and he who had attempted to kidnap me. That man maintained a stoic demeanor despite the pain he must be feeling.

Bafa leaned down and whispered to the king for a few seconds, gesturing toward our prisoner. Arierona nodded and the man was led away, probably to receive attention for his wounds. "We'll leave questioning to the morning," said Bafa as he returned to us. "You might want to be there." He meant me, of course.

Then he lowered himself to the floor and motioned us to do the same. I would have preferred a mat over bare wood, but so be it!

"Welcome back to my house, Lady Teme," said King Arierona. His eyes went to she who sat at my side.

So I spoke words of introduction. "This is Lady Rahiniti, daughter of Temani'itu."

"Ah, she whom he adopted." Arierona sat looking at the diminutive woman for a moment. "I have wondered how this came to be."

Rahiniti spoke up. "He felt I was sent to him just when he decided to leave the sea, so he would not be alone in his house. This my father told me, sir."

"Hmm, that sounds like Temani'itu, to see omens and signs in all that happened." He shrugged. "So he was. I grieve with you for your loss, Lady Rahiniti."

"Thank you, my lord," she murmured.

"All of you I welcome. There are those who will find you a place to sleep and there is always food on the corner porch. Teme knows this well!" he said, chuckling. The king rose to his feet, not so easily, I noted. Arierona was growing older. "We shall feast tomorrow night," he promised, turned, and disappeared into his house.

"He is very formal, is he not?" asked Rahiniti as we, too, rose.

"Arierona is noted for his restraint." And sometimes criticized for being aloof.

"Then we must spend our time with his handsome son," she declared, turning her eyes toward Bafa. For a moment, I felt jealous with no real reason.

ARROWS OF HEAVEN

"Right now, I would like to spend some time with a food bowl," I told her. "Follow me!"

17. Prisoner of War

"I have been defeated and taken in combat," stated the man. "My obligation now is to you as my new master."

He might have claimed this so he would not be executed as a criminal. But it had to be admitted, it might be better to accept his stance as a prisoner of war and gain his cooperation.

It was clear Arierona did not wish to. "I am not at war," he declared, "and I know not what lord you served." The king looked to his adopted son. "It was Bafa who captured you. I leave it to him to decide."

It was not really Bafa but I was not going to argue the point. His men admittedly pulled our prisoner out of the Pool of the Moon.

"I make no promises," said Lord Bafa, drawing himself up and almost looking noble. "Speak and perhaps your words will please us." Well, he did *sound* noble — like a noble in an epic tale, not a real one! "First, how did you know to wait at Pana'a?"

"Why ask so simple and unimportant a question?" I whispered to Toare, the only of my companions to come to Arierona's council chamber with me this morning.

He had an answer. "He starts with easy questions to get the man talking and trusting. Then Bafa can more easily move to the difficult ones, those where our captive might be inclined to hold his tongue."

That sounded good but I did not know if it was true.

"We overheard the women talk of swimming in the pool so we waited there for them," was the answer. The prisoner stood erect, his face impassive, his left arm in a sling.

Bafa nodded rather amiably. "What do we name you?"

The man seemed less sure of answering this. "Loatua — I am Loatua." He paused and then added without being asked, "A warrior of the north, I am."

"Ah, you must have been in the wars."

Loatua nodded. "I served Mahutunoa. Once."

"But no more. Times of peace can be hard for a fighting man."

A hesitation. "Yes, my lord." Bafa regarded him in silence for some seconds and the man began speaking again. "My comrades and I served a minor noble for a while. Then, um, a man we did not know made us an offer."

"You did not know? Was he noble?"

"I think so, my lord. He kept himself covered." So none could read his tattoos. That was possible but it could also be a complete lie. Bafa looked as if he were not sure either, raising one eyebrow oh-so-slightly.

"Why did he want Lady Teme?"

Loatua looked nervously side to side before replying, as if seeking an answer hidden away in some corner of the room. "I don't know and — and I think he was just a messenger for someone else."

"So you know not whom you served yet you claim to be a warrior taken in battle? That sounds more like an outlaw," Bafa accused.

There was no good answer. I could see very well why Arierona turned this over to Bafa. The king and his nephew Ponu who sat beside him — his likely heir — could not hide their looks of approval. Much alike those two appeared, neither more than ordinary in height, of stocky build and with thick eyebrows that nearly joined above their noses.

"Speak if there is anything else you can tell us," he told the prisoner, his voice now not at all friendly.

"Only, my lord, that we were hired in the lands of Mahutunoa but our, uh —"

"Your contact?" hazarded Bafa.

"Yes, exactly, our contact came south too and gave us more directions."

"And you do not know where he might be."

Loatua only shook his head. Bafa motioned to the pair of guards to take him away, and dropped to a mat, just below Arierona's dais, smiling. I had always known there were two Bafas, the amiable and seemingly lazy young man — what Taona Marareta called a 'fop' in the tongue of his homeland — and the blade within that sheath. He raised his head and addressed me. "What do you think we should do with the man, my Teme? The offense was against you."

"Send him to my brother," I responded immediately. I had already decided that would be a good idea.

Bafa turned his head to his father, wordlessly asking his approval. "Let it be so," spoke Arierona, rising, "and so it is settled. I need breakfast." With that he hurried from the room. Ponu, following after those who had taken the prisoner, hurried off as well in the opposite direction.

But Bafa remained to speak with us. "We have learned little," he said.

"Or nothing," I replied.

Toare disagreed. "At least we can be fairly certain whoever was behind it is from the north."

Bafa gave him an indulgent smile. "Or wished us to think so."

"The north is a good place to recruit such men," I said. Both nodded in agreement.

I went on. "But why kidnap me? What would be the reason?"

"That is the central question, the one on which all else rests here. If someone saw you as a rival, naming no names," Bafa said, clearly meaning Ma'ave, "kidnapping would be to no purpose."

Murder would be more to the point. We did not need to voice that fact.

"Then it must have been to extort the High King," said Toare. "Make Teme a hostage."

"That is possible," agreed Bafa. "Likely, even. Or," he added, giving me a grin, "maybe Loatua fell in love from afar with the sister of the High King and intended to take her home with him."

"Ah, I could see the many children," spoke the young bard. "Alas for his unrequited passion!"

"As Arierona, I would rather see some breakfast," I sniffed. "Let us find some and put Loatua out of our minds." And so we did.

But several days later a messenger told us Loatua had sickened and died on his journey to the High King. Some suspected he had taken poison.

18. At the King's House

"I must swim in this lake, too," declared Rahiniti. "It is the biggest pool I have ever seen."

"And are ever likely to," I told her.

"Hito said there were larger ones over the mountains."

"Oh, Hito says many things!" But Marareta and Rika and Aranu had also told me of the great lakes over there and of the river, even greater than the Gurang, that flowed through the vast valley they had visited. The Gurang — "You have seen the Gurang, haven't you?" I asked her.

"We followed it home," she replied. "Or Hito followed it home and I followed Hito. This was not yet my home."

"I would like to see it someday." Yes, I would.

"Your Teoma is large enough for me," was all Rahiniti had to say of that.

"Well, come on," I said, walking toward A'auwa. "You can even leave your loincloth on!" But I didn't, doffing it before diving into the lake. She waded in beside me, still wrapped.

"That is the Sacred Isle, right?" Rahiniti was gazing toward the wooded island, the house of the prophetesses barely visible above its low cliffs. It lay not too distant; I could swim out easily enough, I thought, though I had never attempted it. Didn't the priestesses occasionally?

"It is. Women are permitted to visit but rarely do." I could think of no good reason to.

There were many canoes on A'auwa this morning, some those of fishermen, some bearing women and men across the lake, or up and down its shores. The raft that crossed once each day was about to pull away from the bank some distance below us. It would return in the afternoon with goods and people. Some waited for the raft to ferry them and some chose to walk to one end or the other of the lake and cross the bridges suspended above the Teoma. It could be done in a day.

We might do that later. Today, we should not stray from the House of Arierona and miss the king's feast! Rahiniti and I splashed a while, oblivious to all else, until I spied a woman with a pair of children on the shore. "Amirea!" I called.

She waved and then leaned down to say something to the little girl beside her; her other child was in Amirea's arms. The girl threw off her loincloth and ran down to join us in the water.

The older child would be over four now, and the other less than a year. She swam strongly for her age, but was bashful when she reached us, standing in the chest-deep water — her chest — and staring at Rahiniti.

I have to say that chest-deep water on Ve'emiti rose fairly high on Rahiniti as well. "This is Lady Rahiniti," I told her. To my companion I said, "I present Ve'emiti, the daughter of Amirea and Aranu."

"I greet you, Ve'emiti," said Rahiniti, and turned her eyes toward the land. "This is the famous archer?"

"The best there is," I admitted, "when shooting at a straw target." I did not think Amirea could bring herself to release an arrow at any living creature.

She nodded. "I must see a match between you." A moment's thought led her to add, "And Bafa, too."

I laughed. "Bafa has been humiliated too many times to agree to that!"

Amirea had seated herself on the grass, in the shade of the tall pines that stood lakeside. These were not the old wild trees that grew at the south end of A'auwa but the sort that had sprung up when those were gone. Arierona prized their straight trunks and quick growth, as had the kings who came before him, and they provided the posts and beams of many houses.

We joined the wife of Aranu in a few minutes. "Hito served your husband, did he not?" asked Rahiniti.

"Do not say that to him!" objected Amirea. "He did not serve Aranu but served under him."

"It was Arierona he served," I added to this.

"Oh." She nodded slowly. "And now he serves a god."

It was so. We lazed and gossiped there for a while, and Ve'emiti napped and the baby fussed and we all grew hungry. "We shall see you this evening," I said as we parted. "Aranu will be there, will he not?" He could be out on patrol somewhere.

"He will," promised Amirea. "Who knows, maybe Hito will find his way over here. Or even Pana'a." For only a moment she seemed to reflect on something. "The priestess does not leave her isle so much anymore."

Sometime later, as we visited Arierona's porch to take the edge from our hunger, Rahiniti asked, "Amirea is of the same people as Bafa and Marareta, is she not? She seems much darker." Bafa remained rather pale, the taona not so much, but Amirea had become quite brown when she adopted the life of a Mora woman.

"Those who come from the sea varied greatly. One looked much like your own people." I meant Samua, since gone to the gods. "And one of those who dwells now at the trade village is as dark as a Diwarna."

"Ah. Her father Neatanu is dark too." I hadn't been sure she knew the relationship between the two.

I looked out upon the king's gardens. "I think it would be pleasant to nap beneath one of Arierona's hibiscus," I said. Some were as big as trees. "We must be rested for a night of feasting!"

And rested from our long journey. I still felt the fatigue of that effort. Much of that slipped away in the cool shaded bowers of Arierona's garden.

Once, as daughter to a minor noble I would have been well down from Arierona's place at any feast. Since my brother had become the most important man in the world, that had changed! Yes, in the world. Are not the Mora the most important of all peoples and is he not their king?

It is true that my mother Rahina is Ari Noe, a High Noble, with royal blood in her veins, and I the same. Otherwise, Poneiva could never have been chosen High King.

Rahiniti was of high rank too, of course, so we ended up seated together, she just to my left. I admit I made sure this would be so beforehand. So now we were seated to the left only of Arierona's wife. Amirea, I am afraid, had to take a place well down the line.

Among those between us was Pana'a, the prophetess, the high

priestess of the Sacred Isle. Still a handsome woman she was but I could see gray amid the black in her thick hair. We had not time to speak that night, and she slipped away early, before the storytellers began, but Pana'a did come by our place to lean down and whisper, "We must go visit Hito in the morning." Then she disappeared into the House of Arierona.

19. Across the Lake

"You are not going without me!" declared Toare. "If only for protection. I should have informed Ruiru of what you intended."

I was thankful he had not. Nothing against my bodyguard, you understand, but I would rather not see him this day.

"I was hoping you might invite Toare," Pana'a said to Rahiniti and me. "But knowing you might not, I did."

It was barely dawn, and A'auwa lay misted before us. "The canoe is large enough for all four," she continued, and smiled. "It would have been crowded had you included Ruiru."

"If we decide to walk around the end of A'auwa someday, I will inform him," I announced and slipped into the craft, taking the bow position. It was a broad dugout and, as most canoes used on river and lake, had no outrigger.

We stroked out onto the calm water. "Does it take very long?" asked Rahiniti. She sounded slightly apprehensive.

"Not on a fine morning like this," replied the priestess. "We may have to paddle against the wind on our return." Past her isle we glided, and out into the open water. I had never spent much time on the lake, despite living near it, and had never before paddled across.

"Hoka's shrine is among those trees." Pana'a pointed to a distant wooded shore to south and east, and sighed. "Old Hoka will not live much longer. Then Hito must decide whether he will become the priest of Teva's shrine."

I might not have paddled over but more than once had I walked around the south end of A'auwa and been among those glades. I knew Hoka.

"He will," said Rahiniti with much certainty. "Hito has always journeyed toward this."

"Perhaps," was all the priestess had to say. The sun was breaking through and a light breeze now set the water sparkling. Fish eagles swept above the surface of A'auwa, and carried their catch back to those same trees that were our destination. It was no more than mid-morning when we brought the canoe to a shore where several others rested.

Many shrines were set among these woods, some more visited than others. That of Babi, the Earth, Mother of All and wife to Rai, the Sky, was maybe the most popular. Her priestesses tended to see the moon goddess Pana'a served as only a foolish girl who flirted with Rai as she passed through the heavens.

Naturally, those who revered Marahina claimed that she was his true love which was why he kept her close. And both, I think, were not very serious about any of it.

As we approached the shrine of Teva, I noted that it appeared more well kept than once. That could only be the work of Hito; Hoka ever did little more than sit at his entry, drinking wine and conversing with visitors. That there was often much wisdom in those conversations must be admitted.

A new wooden image of the god stood near the path through the forest. The old one had been splitting from being out in the rains of many seasons. Beyond lay the priest's hut, beneath a spreading forest plum, flowering vines twisting up the walls and over the roof; it looked no different. Indeed, Hoka looked no different, reclining on his bench. One of his wives was moving about, doing something. Ah, feeding their flock of red and gold chickens.

When those plums overhead ripened, I knew, there would be wine. Oh, truly there was always wine, made from whatever fruit might be in season. A figure stepped from the entryway, turning toward us. I think he did not recognize his visitors at first, except maybe Pana'a.

"Tamba!" He stood gaping for a second. "I knew not you were coming."

A moment later the two were embracing. Was there passion in that embrace or was it only joy at seeing one who once was loved and remained a friend? Ask not Teme!

Then he stepped back and looked at her. "I was not sure they could get you to cross A'auwa. Well do I remember your dislike for large bodies of water."

"Never again will I go on the sea," she stated. "Even with you! But I decided this lake is only like a river, but a little wider."

That was true. A'auwa was a part of Teoma's flow. "A sensible girl," remarked Hoka, giving her a full up and down. It was not only her common sense the old priest was admiring.

"Taona Hoka, this is Rahiniti," said Hito.

"The girl you found on the other side of the mountains. Hito has told me much of you," said the priest. "Would you care for some wine?"

I think maybe Rahiniti was a bit disappointed by the shrine, by Hoka, even by Hito. She had served in the great Kohari temple of the Sun Bird, had known the powerful Mora priests who surrounded my brother. This was only a small lonely shrine to a minor god.

"You both serve Teva," she stated, a little tentatively, as we settled down on mats and logs, bowls of wine in hand. "It is good to have a patron god, I think." Then she turned to Pana'a. "And you are a priestess of the moon."

"It is so," agreed Pana'a. She sat regarding me for a little while. "Teme needs a patroness of her own," she said.

"Is there a not a goddess of battle?" asked Hito, with a completely straight face. "Nevatanga, isn't it?"

I had to laugh at the idea. In the stories, the goddess was big and strong, with a voice of thunder, and carried a tree as a club. Moreover, her father ruled over the dead, and she and her handmaids carried the slain warriors to him.

Old Hoka laughed as well. "Surely there could be a better patron for our lady of arrows." I think I liked that title.

"The Kohari archers reverence Balanganay," spoke up Rahiniti. "His bow is seen in the sky after the rains."

"Ah, we also have a god of the rainbow, Wenatu. He is brother to Teva." The priest looked quite thoughtful as he took another deep draught of his wine. "Wenatu would do well."

"I thought he walked upon the rainbow," I protested. I had never heard of gentle Wenatu as an archer!

"A bow is a bow," stated Rahiniti. Hoka nodded in approval of her logic, though he might have agreed with anything a pretty girl said.

A paunchy middle-aged man whose tattoos proclaimed him a

priest of Longo wandered into our gathering a few minutes later. "I wanted to let you know that there has been a group of men skulking about for a couple days. They don't seem to be worshipers. No one knows what they are up to!" He looked at our bowls. "Any of that left, Hoka?"

"There is always wine," declared Hoka. "It is a miracle of Teva!"

"That is why I have to abandon my god every now and again," said the priest, taking a seat. "All they talk about is sex over at Longo's shrine."

Toare leaned close to me. "It might be the kidnappers again. We shouldn't have come!"

"Or we should have brought Ruiru. But we did neither and so it is."

Pana'a had noted our whispered conversation. "You think it might be those who attacked you before?" she asked. Of course, the priestess would know of that, being in the confidence of her brother-in-law Arierona. "Remember Hito was warrior and hero before becoming a priest. You are safe with him."

This must be explained to Hito then. For that matter, we told the entire tale of our travels here, the events at the Houses of Temani'itu and Marareta, on the river, at the Falls of Pana'a. Toare would have told it all, in long-winded bardic fashion, had I allowed him. As it was, both Hoka and our visiting priest fell asleep before we finished.

At the end, Hito nodded his head. "I shall return to Arierona's house with you. I meant to come anyway." He smiled in Rahiniti's direction.

84

Hito did still look like a warrior, despite the life he now led, not a large man but lean and muscular as ever. And he had been not just a warrior, but a man who commanded warriors. There was a shared meal — and more wine — when Hoka awoke from his siesta. The old man listened to Hito's words and grumbled good-naturedly, "He is always running off here and there and leaving me. But he carries Teva with him. This I know."

We saw no one as Hito accompanied us through the forest to the shore of A'auwa. In two canoes, we crossed back to the House of Arierona before the evening lamps were lit.

20. Brothers and Sisters

Ruiru was upset when we returned. "I almost began walking around the lake," he reported, "except I was afraid you would be back here by the time I got over there."

"So you won't feel so useless," I told him, "you can come along when I visit my parents."

"That is a day to the southwest?" He nodded. "I'm ready."

"In a couple days," I laughed. But as it was, we did not need the protection of Ruiru, for my brother Beka arrived that day, with a small troop. With him, too, were his wife and Poneiva's, and all their children.

"When messengers came telling of your encounters," he said, "it was decided that I should come. Of course, Miruhata and E'eva felt that this would be the perfect time to also come and visit." The women had grown up in the House of Arierona, cousins to and closest friends of Rahaita, so it was natural they would wish to return from time to time.

I would still go to my parents' house eventually. I did promise to check on Andarua's coffee trees, after all.

Not unexpectedly, Rahiniti spent much of her time the next few days in the company of Hito. I am certain they did not become lovers again but I might not have been surprised if they had. Bafa, too, was with Hito much. "We have become friends since he returned to A'auwa," was all Bafa had to say. "I visit the shrine sometimes. His life there interests me. And — well, the metals, you know."

I did know. It sometimes seemed the most important thing in Bafa's life. He would spend long hours melting the stones that were brought to him, and seeking out more, or at least rumors of where they might be found. It was the same quest that got Hito in trouble when he went off searching for stones along the Gurang.

Only luck brought him back to the Mora. Well, luck and the fact that he was Hito.

One day Bafa brought me some little gray pellets, maybe a bit larger than the eggs of the fat doves my father raised. "We wouldn't want to show these to Toare," he warned. "This is a metal named lead and I have made these to throw from a sling instead of stones. Feel how heavy!" He plopped one into my hand. Yes, it was heavy and, yes, Toare shouldn't see it. "I have found a source. It was Hito who gave me the idea! And if we don't use them in slings, they still make excellent weights for fishing nets."

I suppose one could become enthusiastic about such things. But why Bafa would want sling-throwers when he had trained the best company of archers in the world, I could not see at all.

More time I spent with E'eva and Miruhata. They were as sisters to me even before they married my brothers. I am younger than they and had followed them about some, I admit, whether they wanted me or not! Of Beka I saw not so much, for he was always conferring with Arierona and Ponu and even Aranu.

But the two women had a protective attitude toward me — this I knew. More than once had they attempted matchmaking for their 'little sister.' Never mind that I was a grown woman now, and taller than either one of them. This time, they seemed to have fixed on

Toare for me.

Which was undoubtedly a terrible match, in nearly every way. Toare was only a storyteller, even if he was the son of Lord Hareata. The boy seemed to have lost his infatuation with Rahiniti. This is not to say she was not sometimes on his mind. "She spends all her time with Hito," he complained.

"He returns to his shrine tomorrow," I reported. "Then she will be all yours again."

He shook his head sadly and definitely too dramatically. The gestures of his trade must become part of one in time. "No, Rahiniti will never be mine. I can see this. And —" He hesitated, giving me a quick glance from beneath furrowed brows. "And she is often with Bafa, whether Hito is there or not."

That I had not heard before. It was not a bad thing, was it? "I think it is time I took Rahiniti to visit my parents," I suddenly decided. "We only need to tear Beka away from his politics for a few days."

Toare laughed. "You know as well as I your brother has little interest or skill in politics. There is probably more drinking than discussion in his meetings."

I had to admit to that truth.

"Yes," agreed Beka, when I spoke to him. "It is time we made that journey. Bring your bodyguard along. I can't keep an eye on you all the time!"

21. Among the Fields

"Nanarul!"

Rahiniti turned to me. "Archer?" Nanarul was a word from the Kohari.

I nodded. "So my father's servants have come to call me," I told her. "We have many Kohari, both slave and freed, here." I waved a greeting to the man who had called out from the field we passed. There was fresh green sprouting from the earth but it was not yet tall enough for me to recognize the crop.

It is nearly a journey of a full day to the House of Amapa for me, on my own. With families and servants and a troop of warriors along, we had broken the trip into two days. I did not mind being on the road again with Rahiniti, nor camping in the open — though it had become more rainy. We had fresher food with us this time and no Toare, who had remained at the House of Arierona.

I had steadfastly refused the suggestions of E'eva and Miruhata that I invite him.

"You need not be very formal with my parents," I went on. "Father is the most modern of modernists."

"Even more than Temani'itu was?"

"Hmm, I suppose not. Your father had less regard for tradition than any Mora I have ever known." Too much so, maybe, but I would not say that to her.

The introduction was brief; there was too much going on with the arrival of son and daughter and daughters-in-law and, of course, grandchildren, for my parents to pay her more than a few seconds of attention.

As we settled into our room — we once again shared a chamber — Rahiniti commented, "I like your mother. And she is not too tall!" This was so; the Lady Rahina was diminutive by Mora standards, though still taller than Rahiniti by the width of my hand. "We share almost the same name," my friend added.

True. Mother's name was not an uncommon one. I am sure I knew three or four women called Rahina. But only the one Rahiniti!

"Is this your room?" she asked. For a moment I did not understand the question.

"Oh, no. I have never named a room as mine. What belongings I keep here are rolled up and put in a storeroom when I am gone." Even in the house of the High King I had tended to switch my sleeping quarters frequently, sometimes nightly.

Rahiniti seemed to wonder at this but said nothing, so I went on. "When I am married, I suppose I will have to settle in one place, so my husband can find me," I told her, trying to look as serious as I might.

But she knew it for the jest it was. "Or move so he can not!" A thought came to her, of a sudden. "What if you had two husbands? I know some Mora noblewomen do."

"I would give each his own house," I replied, "and travel back and forth." I had to giggle at that thought. Me with two husbands? I wasn't sure about having even one.

"Bafa needs a wife," said Rahiniti, quite unexpectedly. "You liked him once, didn't you?"

"When I was just a girl," I admitted. She nodded, saying no more but appearing pensive.

So I said, "The evening meal should be ready. Let's go." And we did.

I had intended to sneak out while my companion still slept, the next morning, and go into the fields with my bow, but she awoke. "Is it time for breakfast?" came Rahiniti's sleepy query.

"If you wish. I was going to go look at Andarua's trees and, ah, maybe just wander a bit." I wanted an hour or two to look at my home. I had long been gone.

"You must take Ruiru with you," she said. Or was it a command? It almost sounded like one. My brother must have told her she should insist on it. "He may be up."

He was, and sitting on the front porch with a basket of cold yams. We shared those as we stepped out into the grayness of dawn. I didn't really mind sharing this walk with them too. I didn't mind having companionship. Why were we stopping?

Rahiniti had halted and stood looking back at the house, its thatched peak touched with gold from the sun rising over the mountains. "This house is like you," she said.

I turned and looked, trying to see what she meant. As I puzzled, Ruiru chose to add his agreement. "So it is."

The House of Amapa, the house in which I had grown up, was different in appearance from most of those she had seen further north. It was rambling and lower in roof, and set in the open fields rather than surrounded by trees and gardens of flowers. It was a house for a farmer, not a ruler.

"Practical, you mean?" I asked. "Or ugly?"

The two looked at each other. "None would ever call you ugly, Lady Teme," stated Ruiru.

Rahiniti smiled. "Except maybe Pua's daughter." Ruiru laughed at that; it seemed he knew of Ma'ave.

"Nor is your father's house ugly," he added. "There is something to be said for unadorned beauty."

"So Ruiru is becoming a poet too," I laughed, and we walked on. But that bit about 'unadorned beauty' stuck in my head. Did Ruiru mean me?

We had planted two little orchards of the coffee trees, well separated so a disease that might attack one would be not so likely to afflict the other. Nor any other sort of accident. They looked well but I knew nothing of how healthy coffee plants should appear. My duty was done.

The fields of my father lay about us. Here and there stood groves of trees, not that tall for the most part. Workers were beginning to appear; at this, the start of the rainy season, much cultivation would be taking place. I led my companions on, bow in hand and quiver on back, with no particular destination in mind. Only walking for a while over these familiar hills would be enough.

It was Ruiru who caught sight of them from the corner of his eye, slipping through a field of millet stubble, left from the last harvest. Three men, and they carried spears.

My bodyguard had naught but a small knife. "Halt!" he cried. Instead, they rushed toward us.

Two things I did. First, I called loudly, once again voicing a war cry. Second, I nocked an arrow, drew back my bow, and stood ready. I did not think of any of this; I simply did it.

On they came and I released the shaft. Another was on my bow a moment later, but the two remaining men had stopped, staring at their fallen companion. I had struck him fully in the chest.

Other men were now rushing in our direction, servants of my father, grasping digging sticks and flint-edged sickles. Most of the Kohari here were former fighting men and most were loyal. Most liked me well enough, too! The two turned and ran. I considered sending another arrow after them, aimed it but then slackened my string and lowered the bow.

Only once before had I actually slain a man. Had I again? The thought twisted about in me for a few seconds.

"Catch them," called Ruiru to the farmhands. I did not think they would be able; the escaping men had a good start and seemed fleet of foot. The bodyguard walked over to he who lay crumpled, knelt down and shook his head. "Dead," he said, barely loud enough that I might hear it.

22. Making a Choice

"No luck in finding them," reported Beka. "They were knowledgeable in ways to hide their tracks."

"There may have been a canoe hidden in one of the streams," added the warrior at his side. Many small waterways crossed our land, all flowing toward Teoma above A'auwa. "We could go down to the south end of the lake to see if they appear."

"They would abandon the canoe before they got that far," I stated. Even I could guess that.

"So they would," agreed my father. "It seems you did not need your bodyguard at all." It was hard to read Amapa's expression but I think there was approval in it. And concern.

"But I am glad you took him," said Beka. "How does the little one?" He meant Rahiniti.

"It didn't bother her much," I reported. "She has seen far worse." We all had heard the tales.

Miruhata and E'eva had to fuss over me after that, alternating between disapproval and admiration. They took turns as to who expressed which, though the wife of Poneiva had ever been the more openly emotional of the duo. Miruhata liked to hide her feelings beneath a sardonic wrapping at times. "We must get you back to the House of Arierona soon," she felt.

"And married," chipped in E'eva. "Then you won't need to run around the countryside shooting at men."

"It might be a good way for her to capture one," Miruhata quipped. I would rather not think about it. What I had done was still heavy within me.

And I carried it with me to my sleeping chamber, where awaited my companions of the morning, seeming in deep conversation of their own when I entered. "I should have carried a spear," said Ruiru, in self-accusation.

"And what difference would it have made?" asked Rahiniti. I think she put too much trust in my abilities.

"It could have made much difference," I told her, "If things had gone only slightly other than they did. It is good to be prepared and now Ruiru will be."

He bowed his head to me in thanks for the words. "I would doubt another attempt now," he said.

For a time, I said only to myself. Whoever was behind it might regroup, recruit more men, and try again. And still we had no idea why.

No need to concern myself over that. I was at my parents' home, surrounded by many of those I loved and who loved me. I would be safe. If I brooded a little over the death I had sent flying from my bow, it was to be expected. One should not be casual about such things.

Hadn't I had acted as any warrior might? People sometimes called me 'warrior,' did they not? Hito had joked of it. I did not mind. I liked being Teme the Warrior, Teme the Archer. Nanarul. The Lady of Arrows, as Hoka had named me. But was I to be no more?

I put such things, such thoughts, aside and shared the evening meal with family, with my friend Rahiniti, and laughed with them and listened to a third-rate bard give us a story. All that was good.

But as I lay down to sleep, I said a prayer to gentle Wenatu, the god of the rainbow and maybe the archer, and asked him to be my patron, to guide my arrows and to bring me rest after. I slept soundly and this I took as a sign.

So it was the next morning, after breakfasting early on fruit and cold meat, I sought out the old woman who drew the tattoos for those in the House of Amapa and asked for the emblem of Wenatu.

"Once," she said, cracking a toothless smile, "we would have asked your father's permission for this. But you are grown tall, my Lady Teme, and know what gods you would serve. It is between you and Lord Wenatu only." She turned her artist's eye on me. "Would you like the rainbow all the way across?" she asked, her gnarled finger tracing an arc above my breasts.

"No, not so ostentatious! Here, maybe." I pointed to my left shoulder. "There is room." She nodded and picked up her bone needle. So it was all the world came to know that Teme, sister of the High King, had become a devotee of Wenatu. I have never regretted it.

23. Figuring It Out

We could not stay forever at the House of Amapa. I might have been willing but none others who came with me. Beka would listen to messengers who came, and shake his head, but did not tell me what they said. My wooden-headed brother might have done well to seek my counsel!

At last he said, "We must return," and so we did, all of us. It rained much on the way to A'auwa.

"Soon, we will go back to Poneiva," said E'eva. "I think Beka will too." She looked at me. "What of you?"

I didn't know but did not say so. One place seemed no better than another right then. And what of Rahiniti? No, I had no obligation to the woman but she had become my friend and I would not desert her here. "I think I would stay longer," I told her. "I might even return to the house of my father." It would not be bad to spend more time there, help with the harvest, shoot with the bow, and forget the world.

Sooner or later, however, it would insist I pay attention again.

Toare noted the new mark on my shoulder immediately. "Had not Hoka spoken of this, I would think it an odd choice," he said. "Did you realize our Ruiru was a devotee of the god?"

My face revealed that I had no idea of this. Once again, my companions knew more of the man than I did. "It is so," he went on, "though he bears no tattoo proclaiming it." Being both a commoner and a warrior, it was not surprising that Ruiru would not choose to bear such a mark.

"I wonder if there is a shrine near," I said. I might ask the man if he knew of one. That was of little importance at the moment. Nothing seemed of great importance right then.

So I settled back into life in the House of Arierona and the king made no comment on it. I am certain he would have let me live there forever. Had not I avenged the murder of his daughter?

I could see living by A'auwa for the rest of my life. But, again, what of Rahiniti? We shared a sleeping room but spent less time together outside it. I was more likely to be with my sisters-in-law or with Amirea. Yes, the wife of Aranu and I did shoot at targets to amuse ourselves and, yes, she still had the surer eye and hand. But not by much. Bafa never joined us but Toare, and sometimes Aranu, would also amuse themselves in our company.

An evening. The rain drizzled on Arierona's garden, dripped from the eaves of his south porch and from the ends of the palm fronds that swayed in the wind. There was nothing to do but stare at the gray sky and nibble at a half-finished bowl of sapa berries. They were terribly bland.

"Do you know how old Bafa is?" asked Rahiniti, sitting down beside me unexpectedly.

I did, in fact, for he had told me once. "Eight and twenty are his years." I chewed on another berry.

"Still a young man, then, and with no wife," she mused. "I like Bafa."

So others had told me. "And does he like you?"

"I am not so sure. He never lets one know what he thinks." There was exasperation in the woman's voice.

"Yes, that is Bafa," I remarked. "Unless it is one of his passions, like archery or metals. Then he will tell you far more than you wish to know!"

She thought on this for a short time before murmuring, "I would like to be one of his passions."

Ah. We would speak of it at last. "He could do far worse, my friend."

"But maybe better, too. Who am I but an outcast Kohari?" She turned her eyes to me. "And I would go no further with this if you — if you had feelings for Bafa."

Feelings? Most certainly, but just what they were I could not say. "If I once thought to love Bafa, that is long past. And there was never any love in return." I shrugged, dismissing all this. "I was only a girl then."

Perhaps I convinced her, perhaps I did not. Nor did I necessarily convince myself of anything one way or another. It did not matter; let Bafa and Rahiniti figure it out for themselves.

Two nights later, Rahiniti did not return to our sleeping chamber, nor slumber there many of the nights after. It seemed that she and Bafa had indeed figured it out. But none spoke of marriage. Bafa continued to have his other passions and was more likely to share those with me than Rahiniti.

I would just as soon he left me alone. I felt safe wandering now, though I permitted Ruiru to accompany me. Once we walked all the way around the south end of A'auwa, across the bridge suspended over Teoma where it rushed into the lake through a narrow gorge, and went on to visit Teva's shrine.

Hoka had no idea if there was a shrine of Wenatu anywhere near but he did admire my tattoo. I don't know where Hito was that day, nor did Hoka. He would disappear for extended periods, the old priest said, perhaps only to sit by A'auwa and meditate, perhaps to wander among the villages of the south. He was still searching, still restless, it seemed.

I was restless too and Toare seemed as much at loose ends as I. "I would as soon have returned to Master Ulani," he told me, "but he has not called for me. And my mother is coming. Ulani might be with her."

"She is coming with Taona Marareta, no?"

He nodded. It was morning, and still dry. The sun played hide and seek behind the clouds, and A'auwa lay before us.

"You should use the time to craft a song or two," I told him.

"I can think of nothing to say." The boy pulled at the grass beside him.

"Maybe there is nothing to say," I told him. "We are just two empty pots!"

24. A Rainbow Appears

"My brother Beka, too, waits on the arrival of Marareta," I informed Toare that afternoon. "They will all talk politics, I am sure."

He roused himself enough to ask, "Will you be able to listen in?" Toare had been dozing on the porch, on and off.

I shook my head. "I doubt it. In the House of the High King, no one stopped me. Not usually. Here, it is hard to go unnoticed."

"Arierona's counsel is often sought," he announced, leaving it at only that cryptic statement.

"I am not even sure what his politics are," I said. I should go over to the buffet and find a snack. "He seems a traditionalist but does not appear to favor their party."

"Ulani says he is traditional but not a traditionalist," Toare told me.

That sounded plausible. As my own brother, Arierona tended to moderation in politics. I think that is a good thing in rulers, not that anyone ever asked me. "It is his nature but not his politics," I said.

Toare nodded. "Even so. Now that we have solved the political situation, we must tackle some other weighty problem."

"No," I objected. "That was enough thinking for one day. Why don't you go get me something to eat?"

He stared at me most insolently. It was a dramatic gesture, of course, and in fun. "Who am I, your husband?"

"Not anytime soon, Apprentice Toare. Maybe when you are

called 'taona' by the people."

"When I am famous, I can pick among all the beauties of the land!" But he got up then and came back with bowls in each hand, and another in the crook of his arm. "Beer," he announced, "and cactus fruit. I wasn't expecting that at this time of year."

"One would have to go into the dry hills for it. Oh, we should do that sometime so we are not so bored. All the way to the Salt Coast!" I gave him a wink. "Thank you for bringing it, Toare. Maybe you would make a good husband after all."

He seemed dejected, of a sudden. "For someone, maybe."

I looked sharply at him, maybe too sharply. "Are you still thinking of Rahiniti?"

He said nothing so I assumed it was so. "I don't like her being with Bafa either, though I shouldn't mind. We should both get on."

"I know." His answer came soft, barely a whisper. We ate silently for a while. A rainbow appeared, out over the gardens of Arierona. That should have been a good sign but I felt like crying. Instead I just let my head sag against his shoulder. It was good to have him there beside me, that solid well-meaning young man who was also a foolish boy.

I heard him whispering something to himself. A poem. Suddenly I sat up straight. "Was that about me?"

He looked embarrassed but answered evenly, "I have been working on an epic about the war. Master Isa said I should and Ulani, um, didn't object." A slight smile. "Ulani would never object to anything Isa said."

"Ulani told me that you are a better poet than he. As good as Isa, maybe." It didn't hurt to tell him that, did it?

"He has told me this himself. We are very different, my master and I. Ulani remains in control of his emotions, always polished, ever the diplomat and, it seems, always has been so. I am a clumsy boy who says things he shouldn't."

"But it takes deep feeling to create great poems," I stated. Whether that was actually true, I had no idea, but it was the sort of thing people said!

I looked out into the evening. "I think it has stopped raining. Let's walk to the lake."

He rose and, being a conscientious sort, returned our empty bowls before accompanying me. Yes, Toare always tried to do what was right, even in the little things. I had liked him for that, even when I didn't know him very well.

What sort of impression had I made on him? Wild Teme, the girl who thinks she is a warrior, spoiled by her brother, the High King? No, that was the sort of thing Ma'ave said about me. Toare would not think so.

He made a most unexpected request as we walked across the wet grass toward A'auwa. "Would you teach me to shoot the bow, Teme?"

I looked quickly to see if Toare again jested. He seemed completely serious. "I thought you were a true Mora warrior who disdained the weapon!"

"Yes, fit only for cowardly Kohari," he replied, and now allowed himself a smile. "So it has always been said."

"Come to the practice ground in the morning." I thought on

this, and added, "I will see if I can get Amirea to be there."

Night was spread above A'auwa, and distant lightning played among the clouds.

25. Aiming True

Amirea wore a leather shirt to protect her breasts from the bow string. I would wear one too, for practice, but found it an encumbrance any other time. I did not protrude so much in the front as Amirea.

"I should know of such things, if only so I can speak truly of them in my songs," explained Toare. I suspected his interest went further. No need to delve into that. He grasped the bow, most inexpertly. "Of what is it made?" he asked.

Amirea answered. "Bafa tried out many woods when he was still interested in the bow." His passions had turned to other projects since. "Sometimes combinations of woods."

"Didn't he try out animal hides too?" I asked.

"Yes, and bamboo, but decided in the end that building of a single wood, cured for two or three years, was the best way to go." She thought on that and added, "Or the simplest way, maybe."

"But the proper wood," I had to say. "He tried out many! Yours is made of sapa." Sapa wood was in plentiful supply.

Toare looked at the bow in his hand. "It is long. Longer than those used by Kohari archers."

That was true. No one could say the apprentice bard was not observant. "We hold it differently. The Kohari turn it sideways and draw it back to their chest. We hold these longer bows upright."

"And they pinch the string," added Amirea. "Bafa and I learned to shoot the longbow in another world. In another life." She seemed to think of that life for a moment, as though it were a dream she once dreamed.

Most of our people did not understand that Marareta and his companions came from a different world, believing only that they crossed the sea from some other shore. Pana'a, the Prophetess of the Isle, has explained something of this to me, and that we Mora, too, once dwelt in that world. I have no gifts of seeing but I understand words plainly put.

"Hold it so," I told Toare, and demonstrated.

The practice grounds of Arierona's warriors lay to the west and the north of his house, behind the scattered thatch-roofed homes of the king's servants and retainers. We were not the only archers at the targets, for a troop of Bafa's bowmen — he still was their commander — practiced nearby.

That they laughed at the haphazard flights of Toare's arrows is to be expected. "None of you were better, not so long ago!" I called to them. But I had to laugh as well, a time or two.

"You will learn," Amirea assured the boy. She was a more patient teacher than I. "I was no better when I started. Unlike Teme, who could shoot well from the first time she grasped a bow."

"Oh?" He squinted at me, making his long homely face all the uglier. "Wenatu must have favored the Lady Teme from birth." I do not know how seriously he meant this. It was often so with Toare, I had come to recognize.

Amirea sniffed but said nothing. She yet had her doubts about the gods of the Mora and followed the ways of her lost home in such matters. Old Samua had once lectured me about their god — they had but one! — but I could make little sense of it.

The sun rose higher and the day grew hotter. Clouds, too, began to fill the heavens. At the peak of the rainy season it would often rain mid-morning as well as in the afternoon. "That is enough," I decided. "Amirea has children she is neglecting."

"Their nurses are quite capable," she responded. "Let's cool off in A'auwa first." I could remember that once, when newly arrived in our land, Amirea was as bashful about showing her body as Rahiniti. She and her mother even covered their breasts at first! That was no longer true and she swam as unencumbered as did Toare and I.

Perhaps Rahiniti would someday become a Mora in this too. Who could say? They were two very different women.

Even if they looked a bit alike. Amirea had the same sort of compact body; one could see her father Neatanu's heritage there, as well as in her tanned skin. She was starting to grow a bit fat, however. In that, Amirea had also become Mora!

Then she went her way, to her little girls — not neglected at all but rather spoiled — and Toare and I went ours. Together, and why not? We were both hungry and so we sought food.

"Ho, Ruiru," called Toare, spying my sometime bodyguard in the garden and beckoning to him. "Come up and eat with us."

The man hesitated. Commoners and nobles did not mix, as a rule, here on Arierona's porch; this was one of the ways in which the king remained traditional. It was not prohibited, if we observed a few old taboos, ones that might be disregarded another place.

I waved him up as well. "He should sit on a separate mat, slightly apart from us," I whispered to my companion. This was not strictly necessary, and I had seen it ignored more than once, but it might be for the best.

Ruiru certainly understood it when he joined us, and took the appropriate place, with his own food bowls.

"The Lady of Arrows has been giving me lessons with the bow," Toare told him.

"Rather we should name her Lady of the Loud Voice," spoke Ruiru. "Thrice have we been attacked and thrice has she nearly deafened me with her war cries!"

I did not mind this. "Either is fine with me. And all great warriors have loud battle challenges!"

"Great?" asked Toare. He was using his bard's voice again, and coating his words with skepticism. I did not mind that, either, but laughed and clouted him.

"Great, indeed," said Ruiru, and raised his bowl of beer to me.

26. A View From the Porch

Toare took to practicing regularly with the bow. Perhaps he even got better at it. I knew he already worked with Arierona's warriors many mornings, refreshing the skills he had once learned, before choosing the life of a storyteller. "He is good with the club," one veteran confided to me. "A little too brash and careless to be a good spear-man, maybe."

And we were together much, both at the archery range and elsewhere. Miruhata and E'eva were exceedingly pleased by this. I think Rahiniti barely noticed; she had her own interests.

That, I tried to ignore, as did Toare. Perhaps we were both just trying to look elsewhere and saw each other. Why either of us should actually care of Bafa and Rahiniti and their affairs could not be explained, not to each other, not to ourselves.

Toare could be sulky when he brooded on it. He would probably say I was too but I would deny it! When, exactly, our thoughts went less to those we once desired and more to each other, I could not say. It happened, and maybe it didn't really take all that long.

"Word has come that Marareta and my mother will begin their journey here in a week's time," he mentioned one evening, sitting on Arierona's front porch. One could see the lake from there, although many trees lay between.

"I already knew that," I told him. "Beka informed me." We sat side by side, gazing out toward rain-misted A'auwa. Closely side by side, as had become our way, pressed together but no more. It was enough to have a presence there, without arms and hands becoming involved. This I told myself, if I actually gave it any thought.

"I shall leave, most likely," he continued. "That depends on how soon Master Ulani wishes to depart."

"I hear his mother decided not to come." Toare only nodded. Neither of us had any real news for the other.

"Do you think your mother will really marry Hito now?" I asked. The priest came and went at the House of Arierona but we rarely talked with him.

"She should. They both wish it." He spoke very surely of this. "There is no reason they should not have happiness."

"I can't see her living at the shrine."

He surprised me by answering, "I can. She was married once to a great noble." That would be Toare's late father, Hareata. "Mehetu does not seek that life again."

That I could understand. "I would not care about being the wife of a great noble." I had rejected a king, after all. Well, we rejected each other maybe. "Would you seek a great noble lady?"

"Maybe a great warrior," he said, giving me a grin.

So I put my arms around the boy and my lips to his. Did he expect this? Probably no more than I had!

Or as much as I had. Either way. Anyway, he didn't object and I couldn't. "We have a week before we need think of anything but ourselves," he whispered.

Oh! Was that where this was leading us? I pulled back a little from Toare. "We do," I agreed. Was one of going to rise and start something going?

No, not yet. But we would and it did not matter which, nor

when. For now we could sit here, beholding night over the Sacred Lake, holding each other.

"I think Rahiniti will not sleep in our chamber tonight," I whispered after a while.

"Neither shall we," he answered, and giggled almost like E'eva. I could barely keep myself from doing the same. "And if she does come in, let her. She can see what she missed out on!"

For that, I had to hit him, truly, but I kissed him after. Then, as it did not matter which of us would act, I decided it would be me. "Come," I said, rising.

There is a custom, when privacy is desired in a sleeping room, to place some flower petals — red, preferably, but white will surely do — on the threshold. Such chambers are not very private, it is to be admitted, by their design and their nature, having walls of woven mats. These hang between the beams and posts of which most Mora houses are built. I had no time to plan for the gathering of petals so I hoped closing the bark cloth that hung across the entry would be enough.

But I would make sure to find a supply tomorrow. We would want them, would we not? Rahiniti might not even know this custom; it probably had not been in her experience in the House of Temani'itu. I unrolled her sleeping mat beside my own. I did not think she would object.

And so it was. We Mora do gossip about our lovers but I think I will not.

If Toare does, he had best compose it as an epic.

27. Wedding Plans

Our affair had its tempests, and Toare and I fought. But it was not as I had fought with Revaru and was more likely to end with lovemaking than tears. Yes, tears — I made Revaru cry many times!

Don't listen to his denials of this. Revaru was, alas, without weapons when it came to a match of wits with me, and took all things far too seriously. Perhaps I took advantage of that too often. Perhaps I was even cruel. Toare could hold his own against me. Yes, we were both impractical and given to our fancies, but we also knew when to laugh.

"The taona is here," announced Rahiniti one dawn, carefully making noise outside before intruding on us. We had reached an understanding there. "Your mother, too, Toare."

I yawned, though I had been awake some time and wondering whether to arouse Toare and, well, arouse him. "Anyone else?"

"His attendant Rika and a couple warriors. The storyteller."

Toare was fully awake now. "His mother? The Lady Pua?"

Rahiniti shook her head. "Nor the Lady Panoha." I hadn't expected Marareta's wife to come.

Our visitor remained poised in the entryway. "Hmm, I will let Toare get up and follow the prescribed customs for relieving himself. You Mora are very odd about such things! It is fortunate that Bafa ignores those ways."

Mostly. Bafa did not wish to offend and so was circumspect. "I will see you maybe at breakfast?" the woman said and was away before I answered.

"Things change now," was all Toare had to say.

"Not until they must," I replied.

A large group sat and shared food, not on a porch but on mats spread in the garden. Arierona had not joined them but Ponu was there, and would speak for him. Marareta, I saw, and Ulani and Beka, and some of the king's captains and even the high priest of his realm. Toare started toward them.

"Hold," I whispered, putting a hand on his arm. "Where is your mother?"

The boy shrugged. "Sleeping in, maybe. She'll find us when she wants us."

I did not think much of that attitude. "Go join your master," I told him. "I shall find Lady Mehetu." He gave me a bit of a quizzical look but did as I told him. Which was what he wished to do anyway.

"Over here," came a low voice, as I wandered up onto Arierona's corner porch. Rika beckoned to me. Beyond him sat Mehetu and Hito, sharing a prodigious breakfast. I needed something of that sort myself, I felt.

"I greet you," I said to all, Rika included.

"I'll go get more food," said he. "I know the Lady Teme's appetite is a thing of legend."

Mehetu announced, almost before my rear touched the mat, "Hito came to me last night, as soon as I arrived, and asked at once if I were ready to marry. I was surprised that he wished to hurry now, as we have felt not the need before. But I said yes, of course, and he explained why."

113

"I wish Hoka to say the words of marriage for us," broke in Hito. "He has not long before he journeys to Teva."

Mehetu went on. "Hoka will not be able to come to us at the House of Arierona, so we shall go to his house. To marry at the shrine of Teva is appropriate, I think."

It sounded reasonable. "You will live there?" I had to ask.

"At times," she replied, glancing toward the man she would wed. "There is no need for either of us to be there all the time."

To this Hito added, "And the house will be for the old man's wives, as long as they want to remain there."

Rika returned with as much as he could carry, baskets and wooden bowls piled high with fruit and yams and the flesh of fowls. "I see there is not much of the pottery from beyond the hills here yet," remarked Mehetu. "I must bring some on the next trip." She laughed and added, "Hito left a great pack full of it at the House of Marareta three years ago."

He smiled and shrugged. "It was to make my fortune as a trader."

"How soon?" I asked, wanting to get back to the wedding. It took a moment for either to realize what I was asking about.

"Two weeks, maybe?" asked Hito.

"Or sooner," spoke Mehetu. "We must abstain from each other three days prior, remember." She sampled some of the sapa berries. "I've never cared much for these."

"They're common up here," said Hito. "If abstain we must, then let us, um, refrain from abstaining as much as we can until then."

"The man followed me straight to my sleeping chamber last night," she reported. "He would not let me rest from my trip!"

Something told me she did not really mind this. Then she turned to me and spoke rather seriously. "So, you and my son, I hear."

Of course she would hear. Not so soon, I had hoped! "It is so," was all I could think to say.

"He will be off following his master soon." Mehetu sighed. "Or so I hope. Do not turn him from his calling, Teme; this I ask of you."

Would Toare do such a thing? Oh, yes, he just might and return to the life of a warrior. A warrior wed to the sister of the High King could rise high, far higher than a teller of stories. But there had been no mention of marriage between us. We were lovers and nothing more, for now. Perhaps, as with Mehetu and Hito, it would take three or four years to go further!

No, no, those two had been thinking of more from the start. It was too hard to figure this out and I did not wish to. I must have sat rather long without speaking as I went over this. "I will keep Toare to his craft," I promised. "Now who will plan your wedding?"

28. News Shared

Toare had interesting news as well, when we again found each other. "There was another assassination attempt on your brother," he reported. "Two men drew close enough to attack him."

"Men? Were they captured?" And what of Poneiva?

"One was taken as he rushed forward with a knife. It seems he was one of the fanatics such as we defeated five years ago."

We? You were only a little boy, Toare. But I was only a little girl and I had played my part. And, too, he had lost his father. "It was a distraction, they say, and another came from behind the High King with a sling." He scowled at the thought of a sling-man. "This time, there was no escape and he was cut down. Nor did harm come to your brother."

"You should have said that first," I told him. "I am not one of your audiences, to be baited so with a dramatic finish."

He was truly sorry, I am sure. His instincts and training as a storyteller had gotten the best of him. "So what did they learn of him they captured?"

"Nothing, it seems. Your brother Beka may know more of it now." He seemed reluctant to tell me, "It was not news to him nor Ponu. Messengers had brought the tale days ago."

And didn't tell me? I must let Beka know I did not approve! "I like my news better," I told the boy.

"As do I. It was about time Hito married my mother. We must prepare him for his fasting and cleansing!" This was always an opportunity for the groom's friends to torment him. Beka told me —

and Marareta agreed with his words — that in their home, men feasted and celebrated the night before their weddings, rather than purifying themselves.

In both cases, it seemed, the male friends took charge of things. So that was no concern of mine, but Mehetu was another matter. Would it be appropriate for her to swim at the Pool of the Moon? She was not a young girl, to go seeking blessings for a fertile marriage. Pana'a would know. I must ask her.

Marareta's presence would undoubtedly bring the priestess to the House of Arierona. There was no point in thinking further on it until she came. "You should go see your mother," I told Toare, "before tonight's meal. Oh, and she knows about us."

He nodded rather absently and went off in more or less the correct direction. I must find my 'sisters,' E'eva and Miruhata, and see if they would help plan a wedding. Not that I would ever expect them to say no! But first, to seek out Marareta or Ulani or even my brother and learn more of what went on in the House of Poneiva.

It was both Marareta and Ulani I found, near the lake. "We await Pana'a," came Ulani's cheerful voice. "One of the priestesses said she would come."

"I would speak to her too," I said. I regarded the taona. He yet loved Pana'a; of this I had no doubt. Not as he had Rahaita, not even as he did his wife. It was an old love, a love that had faded, a love of memories and nostalgia, to be reawakened now and then before they returned to their lives. That they would have wed had not Pana'a been bound to her life as prophetess and priestess, I also have no doubt. That could not be.

117

But, in a way, she was wife and he husband. There was a bond and it would last as long as they did. I felt a great sorrow for them for a moment or two, as well as a sort of envy.

"I must have all the news of the north from you," I told them. "When you have time." It would not do to pester Marareta now. Ulani, maybe.

The latter spoke. "I am sure Toare has told you some of it."

"He has. He is off to see his mother now. She and Hito are getting married at last."

Marareta smiled at this. "It was not unexpected. We must have Arierona let them use his gardens."

"No, Taona, they are to marry at the Shrine of Teva. Hoka will join them, as he did Rahaita and you." I had been there. Ah, Rahaita had been so beautiful!

"Pana'a comes," Ulani informed us. Any other words of news would have to wait.

Her dugout slowly approached, gliding across the calm water and into the shadows of the pines. The high priestess was alone this morning.

"Marareta," she said, softly, and embraced the taona. Ulani got only a nod. But to me, Pana'a spoke more words. "You and I must prepare for Hito's wedding. All the priestesses wish to be there." I knew that one was required to always remain on their isle, just in case the goddess visited. "Let us go eat and discuss many things."

It was late enough — past mid-morning — for another meal, so we went to the House of Arierona. But it was not of weddings we spoke, but the events in the north.

First asked Pana'a, "Did the Lady Pua come with you?"

"I asked that Pua accompany us," spoke the taona. "She preferred to settle into her new home and allow her son to represent her." He nodded toward Ulani.

"That is well. I value Ulani's counsel and it may be needed in the time to come." She paused, choosing her next words with care. "We have seen things, we on our isle," spoke the high priestess. "Things that whisper of the Hero from the Sea and what he brings."

"Did not the taona fulfill the prophecy?" I asked. Or maybe Bafa and Beka, with him. They had certainly brought the people their king, as foretold — Poneiva.

"The prophecy has not necessarily come to pass in its fullness," Pana'a said. "There may be one more promise to be kept."

There was no point in asking her what that meant. Prophetesses say such things and it is for us to figure them out.

29. The Falls of Pana'a

"I would ask you to be my protector when I go to the Pool of the Moon, Taona," spoke Mehetu.

Pana'a had assured me it was appropriate, and maybe even desirable, for Mehetu to bathe in the pool below the falls. "There are many blessings that may come from the Moon Woman," she said.

"I would be honored," replied Marareta, smiling. "It will not be my first time."

"Tomorrow, then," I told both. "The moon will be near full and bright." If it didn't rain.

Of course, I intended to go along. I should probably alert Ruiru to that fact. He tried to be unobtrusive but I knew he lurked in my vicinity much of the time.

"And the wedding the next day," I added. "Already is Hito preparing himself." Only by avoiding contact with his bride-to-be for now. Tomorrow he must fast, and spend the evening in the sweat lodge while Mehetu splashed in cool waters.

That attended to, Toare's mother went her way. Ah, Toare! Little time had we spent together since she and the taona arrived. And Ulani — he took up even more of his apprentice's days, and even nights.

With Marareta I walked, wherever he was going. "Taona," I asked, "will my brother be alright?" He knew which one I meant.

"Poneiva is capable and careful," he replied, "but any High King has enemies. Any powerful man for that matter." He stopped and gave me a look. "Powerful women, too, I should certainly say."

He couldn't mean me. "Lady Pua?"

"Yes, and her daughter and my wife and Lady Mehetu and a great many others. They all have their parts in what happens in this land. As do you, Teme."

I stopped and stared at the floor. "Maybe I should go back to my brother's house."

He smiled and we started walking again, down the hall toward Arierona's gathering room. "And give him the protection of your bow arm?"

"Every arm counts in a battle," I said. That was an old proverb. "Is anything known of they who attacked Poneiva?"

"Almost nothing. The man they captured was meant to be sacrificed, to allow the other to attack. He was a fanatical priest recruited by someone, a man who knew nothing except that he had been given a mission by the gods."

"Then the traditionalists are behind it?"

He shook his head. "I doubt it. Parrot or Owl, those of both factions support the way things are done now. It is only a few extremists who would have no High King."

"And those were defeated. The war is over."

"But the reasons for it remain. This we all need to recognize." We had reached the house's high-ceilinged central chamber. "It is late," the taona said. "I shall seek my sleeping mat."

After he left, I wondered if Pana'a would be sharing it. Not that it was my concern. More important was whether Toare would be sharing mine!

I already slept when the storyteller found his way to me. I was quite willing to wake up for him. Who could know how many more such nights we had?

We gathered toward the middle of the next afternoon by A'auwa, Mehetu and I and Ruiru arriving first. A little later, the taona hurried to us. "I had to at least make an appearance among the friends of Hito," he explained. That he was a busy man, we all knew; it was good that he made time for Hito and even better that he made time for Mehetu. He had treated her well after the death of her husband and his great friend, Hareata, allowing her and Toare to remain in the house now given to him.

Mehetu. She was somewhat older than Hito — perhaps ten years? I did not know. Nor was Mehetu a woman of beauty, having the long plain face she had passed to her son. Not ugly at all, mind you, and she was well-made, slim, straight, and tall. Many would admire the way she carried herself as we walked northward.

To the right, A'auwa. We passed the isle of priests, where Samua had sought solitude for a season or two. It lay close above the falls.

We spoke little, each with our own thoughts. Perhaps Marareta thought of when he had walked here with Rahaita, when he had served as protector of Miruhata and E'eva on their wedding eve. I, too, thought of that though I had not been invited along then.

"I shall remain here near the road," said Ruiru, as we began the descent beside Pana'a. The roar of the falls was greater than on my last visit; rain-swollen A'auwa was cascading into the valley of the pool. This mattered little. Perhaps the water was a little higher, the current a little stronger out from shore, but there were safe coves for Mehetu's swim.

I thought I should point them out. "And take your time," Marareta told her. "We will wait." The taona gave her a blessing and Mehetu slipped into the dark water. The moon was low in the sky; the clouds passed before her face.

"Let us give her privacy," said my companion. We walked a short way up the path to the little wayside shrine to Marahina, and settled on the ground.

"I hope Mehetu doesn't need us," I told him. "We would never hear her."

"I sat here once with Rahaita," said Taona Marareta, gazing out into the darness. "We sat at this shrine and talked, as E'eva and Miruhata bathed below." He smiled at a memory. "That night, we could hear them quite well, splashing in the water. I might not have admitted it to myself at the time but I think that is when I fell in love with Rahaita." A pause. I thought maybe he was finished. "And I also think she had already decided she loved me."

I was glad it was dark so the taona could not see my tears, nor I see his. "I hope you can be my protector when I swim here some night," I said.

"I hope not," he answered, "for I intend to be the priest at your wedding."

"Ah. Yes, that would be even better, Taona." I raised myself to my feet, though I would gladly have laid down and slept instead. "I should check on Mehetu."

Where was she? Ah, there, resting close to the shore and gazing up at Pana'a. There was enough moonlight to make out her features.

She had seen my movement and turned to me. "I am joyous that I chose to come here to wed Hito, rather than at the House of Marareta. Every bride should swim in the Pool of the Moon."

"It would get very crowded, I think," I told her. I heard voices, saw figures descending the path. "Here come some more now!"

"Then I shall come out. Surely that was enough, even for a bride my age." Mehetu came ashore, looking about. "Where did I leave my loincloth?"

For a moment I looked, too, before realizing I held it in my own hands. "Here," I said, holding it out.

"Bless us, Taona," came a voice from above us, and I heard Marareta say a prayer for the blessings of the gods. A moment later, two young women were diving into the pool. Mehetu and I climbed to where he waited and then on to the patient Ruiru.

30. The Old Priest

Most came across in canoes, large and small. Some of the priests from the various neighboring shrines walked over and the priestesses of the isle had arrived early in a large canoe — all but one of them, of course. Now the guests sat and conversed before Hoka's house, in the shade of his plum tree, waiting.

I had come with Toare and Mehetu and Marareta in a roomy dugout. Hito was already at the shrine, ferried over as soon as he left the sweat lodge last night — having first jumped in the lake and swallowed some quantity of its waters. It had been Rika who had attended to that chore, Hito's longtime friend, a man who had gone over the mountains and back with him.

Would Rahiniti come? I wondered. If she did, it would be with Bafa. Yes, there both were, and Beka with his wife and sister-in-law. Had there ever been so large a gathering at the shrine of Teva? No doubt the god was looking down and scratching his head, wondering where he had found all these new devotees.

At noon, we had been told. The old priest Hoka preferred that and it gave we who had crossed A'auwa time to cross back before it grew too dark, and attend the feast Arierona had prepared for the couple. I think neither Hito nor Hoka had expected such a crowd.

"I am to escort Hito to the priest," whispered Marareta, when we reached the shrine. "I should go find him." I had already known this. Pana'a had taken the same role for the bride — what would normally be the mother's role, though she was no more than two or three years older, maybe.

"Do they have their crowns?" I whispered to Miruhata.

"Of course. Though Hito wanted to wear the one Lady Pua made Marareta as a priest of Teva, and then was gifted to him." We both knew that wouldn't do for a wedding; even the rather nice one Mehetu wore when her station called for it was not exactly suitable.

Hoka was standing now, with his own feathered crown reasonably straight on his head. "By the statue," he croaked out. Some caught his words and the rest followed them.

One of the old priest's wives stood beside him, to lend a steadying hand. He looked very worn. Hoka had a good life, hadn't he? At least since settling at the shrine. There were odd rumors about who and what had been before then and most agreed Hoka was not his real name.

"I welcome you on a special day," he announced, his priestly voice finding itself. "The wedding of my successor —" He glanced in the direction of his hut. "Or so I hope. Also," he continued, "what is likely to be the last wedding ceremony I shall ever perform. Yes, this I know. I go to Teva soon, or whatever god will have me!" His laugh became a cough. "Hmm, I need some wine so I don't do that during the rites." The other wife brought a bowl.

"So let us begin, here in the sight of Teva, God of Rain and of Love!" First came Hito, in a clean white loincloth — more a kilt, actually — and a high white feathered crown, led by Marareta, who stood aside when they reached the priest. Then Mehetu in an identical costume and Pana'a playing the same role as the taona. Hoka's smile was broad; he seemed the happiest person there!

The rites of marriage are brief. If one did not pay attention, one would not know the words had been spoken and the couple wed. I could not help glancing at Toare during the ceremony. Would we have such a day? He was more interested in watching his mother and never looked my way. Who knows whether he too had such thoughts?

But I also glanced at Bafa and wondered other things. There is no point in speaking of those.

Then Hoka went to take his nap and we all paddled back across the lake. I think maybe Hito did not want to leave the old priest, nor do I think he wished to sit at Arierona's right hand, with his new wife at the king's left, the guests of honor on this night. Ah, Hito was now ennobled, was he not? That too, I am sure he cared not about.

I found myself sitting with Toare and Ulani, as the feasting gave way to songs and dancing and much consumption of beer. "I have put aside the epic on which I worked, for now," Toare confided. To both of us, I guess. "It is better to turn elsewhere for a time."

Ulani nodded. "You can return to it when you are ready. But to what are you turning?"

"Hito's tale. I think maybe we see its end here tonight."

I disagreed. "Not until Rahiniti also comes to some conclusion. The two are — are intertwined."

Toare frowned, even as Ulani laughed. "I fear you are right, Teme, but that shouldn't keep Toare from working on it." He sipped his beer — Ulani never drank deeply — before saying, "Isa is at work on a new epic, the tale of my brother Ve'eta in the civil war. He gave me some of it when I stopped at his house."

"Is there enough there for an epic?" asked Toare. It seemed lacking to me, too.

"A short one. The master feels it will be his last great poem." A pause. "I think he does it in part from gratitude for the boy's kindness to him while he was High King, and partly for my mother's sake."

"Ve'eta was a good man," I agreed. I almost said boy, too, but checked myself.

"But foolhardy," came Ulani's response. "Which is why your brother now stands on the High King's dais."

I think Poneiva will figure in many epics.

Part III. The Shaft Sped

31. Different Directions

"I shall remain here with my husband," said Mehetu. "And he shall remain as long as Hoka yet lives. After that, who knows?"

"My house remains open to both of you. It is your house as well, Lady Mehetu," came Marareta's reply. "The rest of us, I think, shall be scattering again."

I wasn't sure if I would be one of those. Returning to the House of the High King did not appeal to me, nor did anything else, in truth.

Toare would be following Ulani somewhere. It was time he went back to being the apprentice, sharpening his skills, and — most important — being seen with his master. So might he become known throughout the land.

I almost wished I had not promised his mother to keep him to that task. It would be pleasant to live with him in some great house, where he might be a noble commander. Arierona would surely take him on if I asked.

But I could live in the House of Arierona anyway, could I not? Perhaps I would for a while longer.

So went my thoughts when Rahiniti joined me later, as I lazed on the king's porch, considering falling asleep for an hour or three.

"Bafa has no time for me!" she complained. "He and the taona spend all their time with his metals. Your brother, too," the woman added.

All three of them men from the sea, brought to our land as the prophecies had foretold. They knew of things the Mora did not, and those stones were part of that.

"Bafa will always be so," I told her. "Be thankful he makes any time for you." That I regretted as soon as it left my lips.

But Rahiniti did not mind. "We like each other," she mused, "and we have enjoyed ourselves, but I know he does not love me."

I was not sure that mattered, not with those two. She could be a good wife to Bafa, an attentive wife. Ah, but would he be a good husband for her? He might never be as attentive in return, though undoubtedly loyal. "They speak of traveling north to search for their stones," she continued, settling down at my side.

This I found interesting. "To the Gurang?"

"I am not sure. I did not listen that much, for I am interested neither in metals nor in going anywhere." She yawned. "Except maybe to sleep."

She napped still when I rose. The afternoon rains had drenched Arierona's gardens and I, too, felt damp. Hungry, as well, so I made my way to where the food was laid out. Not much choice at this time of day, everything picked over before the evening meal was served. I settled on some cold millet cakes and a scrap of coconut meat. That would hold me.

I did not like the look of much else that was left. It would probably find its way to the pigs soon. I should find my way somewhere,

I thought, as I leaned against a post, holding my bowl and gazing out across the gardens. To Bafa, yes, and learn what sort of journey he might be planning.

Might the taona still be with him? I knew where his workshop was and had visited more than once, a hut off to the south and west of the gardens. It would not hurt me to get wet. But, in truth, I was drenched by the time I reached it and must have looked like I fell in a river.

Taona Marareta was still there, and one of Bafa's helpers. They were crouched near a fire, peering into it and speaking in low tones, as if fearing to disturb something. It was only some of his stones being melted. Men can act most oddly.

Bafa looked up. "We are making bronze," he announced with considerable pride.

"Or attempting it," said Marareta.

"Oh, we will be successful," he was assured. "I have made it several times now and am only trying to perfect my method." This explanation was surely added for me. "If only I had more metal! Tin, especially. Only a bit comes to me from time to time."

"Then go find some more," I told him. I was not about to let him know I had already heard of his plans. I moved closer to his fire, not from interest so much as a desire to dry myself.

Yet I was interested, I admit, and squatted down to peer at the metal placed in the coals with the rest of them. "This is the mixing of copper and tin, is it not?" I asked. I had paid some attention to things Bafa had told me.

"It is, and more useful than either by itself."

131

"Hmm." I stood and looked about the open-sided hut. There were rocks in piles, and some of the metals Bafa had made were placed on bamboo tables. They looked as though they had been hammered on, to shape them, but not a few had broken. "I know the lead," I said, nodding toward a number of the pellets he had shown me. "What is that beside it?" It was pleasantly shiny.

"Silver," Marareta told me. "Bafa has found no use for it."

"This is so," admitted Bafa. "We find it mixed with the lead."

"Make Rahiniti earrings of it," I told him.

The toana liked this idea. "Jewelry is always preferable to weapons," said he. Then he addressed me seriously. "There will be a council in the morning and I think you should be there."

Bafa raised an eyebrow at this but said nothing. "You have worthy ideas," Marareta continued. "It is time others recognized this."

"I do," said Bafa. "The Teme of old was never slow to share them. That has changed some, my girl."

Taona Marareta laughed. "Teme is only learning to be a politician." I stood staring from one to the other. Were they actually being serious?

"But do come sit with us in the morning," said Marareta. "If you have no wish to speak, that is acceptable, but I would like you to hear the words spoken." He glanced toward Bafa. "I do not think the king will be there, but Ponu might. Your brother, and Ulani, too."

"But not his apprentice," Bafa had to slip in.

"No, Toare does not belong yet in such councils. Give him a year or two."

I had to ask. "Of what will you be speaking, Taona?"

He only smiled. "To learn that you must come."

32. A Council Chamber

Looks of mild curiosity greeted me but none objected to my presence. Perhaps the taona had already told them he wanted me to be a part of this meeting. My brother Beka was there, and Ulani, as he had promised, but Ponu did not appear. Aranu sat with us, I think as informal representative of the king.

I fear neither he nor Beka truly possess the skills needed for politics. They are good men and brave warriors. I had no ambition to be more than good and brave myself.

These, with Bafa and Marareta, I thought to be all who were gathering here in this chamber at the rear of Arierona's house. It was a room I liked, on the back wall, with a large window giving a view toward the warriors' exercise grounds. Almost a porch, it was.

Then entered Hito and Pana'a. I half-expected Mehetu to follow her husband — Marareta had spoken well of her capabilities, had he not? But the noblewoman did not appear and servers brought bowls of fruit and beer, lest we grow peckish before we finished.

Pana'a had taken the place to my left. I would just as soon have done it the other way around. It didn't matter much here. To my right was Beka, my brother; as siblings of the High King we did have the highest rank and position. But it was Marareta and Ulani who led this day.

"We have all heard of the latest attempt on Ponieva by now," began the the taona. "There is not much to be said of that nor much any of us can do. Yet I would hear the words of the Lady Pua's son, here as her representative."

Ulani nodded respectfully to him and began. "Who can say what factions might be behind such things? Some would claim even that my mother would stand to gain." He paused for a moment. Yes, there had been mention of this. "My brother was only twelve when his uncle, the High King Maitoa, passed, and was too young to be considered as a successor. It was our brother Ve'eta who stood upon the dais, before he was slain in battle. Now Mouiri is of an age to be considered fit for rule."

All knew this; Ulani was just putting things into words for us. "Not so long as the capable and healthy Poneiva is High King, to be sure. But if there came a choice, the traditionalists would prefer him to his cousin Ikataki, his most obvious rival. Or perhaps the net would be thrown wide again, as it was when Poneiva was chosen — there are many third and even fourth cousins who might be considered."

"Ikataki has made himself a leader among the Parrots," said Beka.

"Yes," agreed Ulani. "There was room for him to do this. I know not how much he truly favors their ideas." From his tone, I suspected he thought the man gave only lip-service to them.

"We know you are with them," spoke Pana'a. "Or at least your mother is."

Ulani shrugged. "I admit to no strong feelings one way or the other, on most policies. But yes, the Lady Pua still has influence among the modernists."

"The fact is," said Marareta, "most of us in this room are not a part of any faction. Our Hito, our Aranu, are old-fashioned but hardly strong traditionalists. Even Teme, who grew up among a flock of Parrots, seems to favor moderation." There were smiles around our circle. Yes, my parents were very much part of the modernist group.

"But Teme herself is not very moderate," Bafa had to joke. "She is quite enthusiastic about things that take her fancy." I had to give him an accusatory stare. "Oh yes, as am I, my lady!" he admitted.

"We must also consider the attacks on Lady Teme," said Ulani, bringing us back to our discussion. "We know not who is involved, nor why."

"Could it be the same individual?" wondered Bafa. "Or individuals?"

"I can think of only one person who would have a great desire to see the last of Teme," Ulani answered. We all knew he meant his sister. "I think we can rule her out."

There were nods of agreement. Ma'ave would gain nothing from a kidnapping, nor do I think any believed it would be in character for her. She could be petty and disagreeable but her plots were all of a political nature.

"Some noble hoping to use her against the High King, I would think," put in Hito.

"Who might or might not be involved in any cause or faction." This from the taona. "We can only hope the scheme has been abandoned."

"But Ruiru will continue to guard my sister," vowed Beka.

"And I think we can all agree that there is little to agree on, one way or another," Marareta said. "We desired only to speak of these things before we each went our separate way. But there is another matter that more immediately involves us." He turned to Ulani.

"There are changes coming in the north," the bard said. "In the trade village where once my mother held sway, and in the lands beyond, where dwell the Diwarna — and others."

Hito had no trouble understanding. "You mean Gordie. Finally putting some pressure on the Mora up there, is he?"

"I understand he's made himself almost a king," spoke Bafa.

"In all but name," Hito agreed. "Subject to no one and growing steadily more powerful."

"It's been five years since either of us saw him," said Marareta. "His path was different from the rest of us, we who came here from the sea, almost from the start." I knew he was the youngest of them, and had taken a Diwarna girl for a wife, remaining in the north, never living with the Mora. Ulani's epic allotted him a couple lines.

"For now," said Ulani, "he has only asked the High King — and quite diplomatically, I must say — that he nominate the new Mora administrator for the trade village." He looked toward Hito. "You know the man well, I understand."

Hito seemed puzzled for a moment. "Not Taki?"

Ulani nodded. "So it is. He seems competent but he is Lord Gordie's man."

"But what of the Lady Ma'are?" Hito asked. "And isn't she related to you?"

"A cousin by marriage," was the answer. "She is originally of some minor noble family from the kingdom of Anana, I believe.

But she has proven herself quite capable, and her husband Heho is a good man too. Poneiva would like to have them closer and they have expressed a desire to again live among their own people, if only for the sake of their children."

Marareta was becoming a bit impatient, perhaps. "What it comes to is that Poneiva wants someone to travel up there and make sure the turnover is smooth. Someone who can talk nicely to Gordie, approve the change, and then escort Ma'are home."

"You, Taona?" I had to ask.

He shook his head. "I should be closer to what is going on here, as should Ulani. We do have a man with us very suited to the task." Marareta turned toward Bafa. "And he could finally talk to Gordie about finding sources of metal along the Gurang."

I may never have seen Bafa so delighted, his grin so wide. "A splendid idea! When should I leave?"

33. Scattering

Messengers were at once dispatched to Poneiva. Many of our friends would soon be leaving as well. Let me say that I had decided as soon as Marareta spoke of an expedition to the north to be a part of it. I think he expected that.

And Beka immediately attempted to say no as soon as he was informed, which was also to be expected. I had hoped he would not learn until the last moment and after he had gone back to my other brother. The taona took my side.

"You are Teme's brother and can object to her plans, but she is an adult so you can not prevent them. Even Poneiva can not without bending the laws. Only the leader of the expedition may prohibit her coming and that would be Bafa.

"Not even Arierona, though Bafa serves him." He didn't mention that the king could, of course, withdraw his support and leave Bafa without warriors. "Teme will be safe with him, and Aranu is going."

"Aranu? He is a good man."

"And he feels comfortable taking his own wife along to visit her friends beyond the hills." I had not heard this before. I wondered if Amirea was bringing along her girls.

But yes, I would be very safe with Aranu and Bafa and Ruiru and a contingent of warriors, including bowmen. Even safer might I have felt if Hito came along. His duty was to the old priest; I understood that.

Toare, of course, was headed another direction with Ulani. Only two days later did we say our farewells. "Do we love each other?" I asked him. He was honest enough to say he didn't know. Neither did I.

"Maybe we can sort that out when I get back," he said. "Or you get back!" Then he was gone, down the road beside A'auwa with Ulani, and Marareta and Rika with them.

Bafa became very busy and very efficient. "We can leave the planning to him," Aranu said, "and to Amirea."

Between the two, they did do a good job. I had no more to do than pack a basket and make sure I had enough arrows. I spent my mornings practicing with those, shooting at rounds until I was too tired to shoot more, impatient to be on the way.

Bafa had never been past the hills, save when he was a captive of the Kohari, much further north. That experience was something he shared with Hito — and with Rahiniti, in a way. What would Rahiniti now do? I did not think she intended to come along but I asked, to be sure.

"I have had enough excitement following you about!" she said. "I will stay in this house, I think, and wait."

"For Bafa?"

"I think not," was all she would say of that.

"I am going over to visit Hito before we leave," I told her. "To-morrow maybe. Would you like to come?" At once, I thought it might be a bad idea, with Mehetu there and the couple newly wed.

"Do we canoe or walk?" was the only reply.

"I will be walking enough in a few days," I told her. "Meet me by A'auwa in the morning."

140

We saw each other again sooner than that. Rahiniti moved back into our sleeping chamber, for Bafa seemed to be too busy for her, and Toare was no longer under foot. "I can have this room to myself when you go," she told me. Then, becoming a bit introspective, Rahiniti said, "I think it will remain so while you are gone."

I suspected we would both sleep alone for some time, even if neither had made any promises.

Lying there in the dark, my mind could not help turning to Toare. He was — what? Only someone with whom I spent a season before I went on? I had but one lover before him; I have told you that. Revaru, impetuous, quarrelsome Revaru.

Rahiniti had known only two lovers as well. Had she not told me so? She might be as lost as I! Now she slumbered peacefully a short distance from me, knowing no better than I what would come. Ah, I should put these thoughts aside. Soon there would be other things to take my attention, a new land to explore.

In time, I too slept.

34. The Shrine of Teva

"You understand the meaning of *Mora*?" he asked.

"I think so." Rahiniti sounded uncertain; the literal meaning was obvious but our language has many nuances.

"Mora is the name of our land but it also means us, for we are one. The land of the sleeping sky, a place of rest after the storm-filled journey that brought our ancestors here." Hito paused and took a sip of his wine. "Hoka's wives are going to teach me the making of this," he said, before returning to our topic.

Hoka himself slept in the sun by his house, his breath rasping.

"It is not something we think of, most of the time." He looked up at his wife, standing beside him. "Mehetu reminded me of it. She is full of old tales and wisdom."

"But not old herself," she reminded him.

"Certainly not." I think that might have been a private jest.

"The sky did not sleep last night," objected Rahiniti. "It growled a great deal."

"The rainy season is coming to an end," I put in. "It will be good weather for traveling."

"That is a journey I have no desire to again make," Hito said. "Definitely not as before with a pack-basket heavy with trade goods! But it might have been good to see old friends."

"Let them come to you," I told him.

It was hard to read the slight smile he gave us. "I have the wisdom of neither Hoka nor Marareta to draw visitors to this shrine."

"Then allow Lady Mehetu to do the talking." The lady seemed

to think this an excellent idea.

I heard a laugh and looked to where Ruiru was gossiping with one of Hoka's wives. One or the other must have said something amusing. It seemingly woke the old priest, who looked about in momentary confusion. "Who is here? Ah, the pretty girls have returned! You should make them stay longer, Hito." He coughed a bit and Mehetu took him a bowl of wine. "Keep this one, too," said Hoka.

"So I intend, Master," was Hito's response.

Hito turned back to us and spoke in a near whisper. "Your bodyguard has expressed interest in the priesthood. It is not unusual; many priests were warriors when younger." That would include Hito himself. "A priest of Wenatu of course. He thinks we need a shrine." He looked at me and added, "It was your adoption of the god that turned his thoughts so. He saw it as a sign."

That was not something I felt like discussing. "He grew up around here, I am told," I said.

"Yes, I knew him when we both served Arierona, before he followed your brother. Ruiru is only a little older than I." He sipped some more wine and turned his eyes back to Hoka. The priest had fallen asleep again. Hito shook his head and continued. "He comes from one of the families that fish on A'auwa."

Mehetu took a seat beside her husband, on one of the sections of log placed near the statue of Teva. I wondered who had carved that image. It was not as exuberant as the old one. Anyone could have seen from it that Teva was a god of love.

"Hito worries about his master," she said, not very loudly.

"He will not be here when you return, this I know," said Hito. "Hoka knows it too, when his mind doesn't wander."

Mehetu stated, "It wanders places we can not go."

"It is so. Marareta suspected this, long ago, and Pana'a too. Hoka has gifts similar to her own. He has always kept them hidden. At least," he added, "since he came here and became Hoka."

I understood this. "A prophetess is one thing but people fear a sorcerer."

"So is it," agreed Hito. "On the other side of the mountains, he might have had a place of honor."

"Or even in the swamps of the Diwarna," spoke Rahiniti. "I met Oorto, remember."

Hito nodded and spoke to me. "Be certain to give the shaman my greetings. I am sure you will meet him."

"Assuredly, Friend Hito." I had never so addressed him before, as do equals. "We should go," I said rising. I saw that Hoka was awake again, and that he looked alert, at least for the moment, so I went to him.

"Taona Hoka," I said, "will you give us your blessing before we go?"

"Go? Didn't you just get here?"

"Lady Teme must travel on a long journey," Rahiniti announced. "She asks the favor of Teva." She smiled most sweetly on the old man. "As do I."

Growing up in a temple probably made the woman good with such things. Hoka looked up at me and his eyes seemed to suddenly see other worlds. He shook his old head and raised his hands, palms

144

out. "I ask the blessings of Teva —" He paused. "Hmm, and of We-natu too, and of all the gods." The old man gave me a wink. "May all journeys be pleasant and destinations welcome."

Then he became deadly serious. "There is a destiny waiting for you, my lady," Hoka said. "I can not quite see it but I know it awaits." He turned from me. "Where did my wine bowl go?"

35. The Road North

Amirea had agonized over whether to bring her daughters along. At the last, she and Aranu decided to leave them with Miruhata and E'eva, even when that pair returned to the House of Poneiva with Beka. It was planned that we would first go there on our return to the Mora lands.

This meant fewer servants and quicker travel, so I was glad of it. Twelve warriors would accompany us, four of them archers. Far from being Aranu's full command! When Hito served with him, he had led a troop of a hundred; now he had advanced to commanding those who commanded such troops. He might be the highest of Arierona's captains before he was done, or some other king's.

So he and Amirea with a couple servants, Bafa and his attendant, Ruiru and myself, the warriors of Arierona — these marched from the king's house that morning, southward. Yes, south; it was simplest to go around that end of A'auwa before heading toward our destination.

Rahiniti waved to us from the porch, and my sisters-in-law, and all the children of three families. I had asked E'eva and Miruhata to keep an eye on Rahiniti, as they could. They themselves might be on the road away from A'auwa soon.

It was a long walk, I knew, weeks on the paths north. All travel by water was decided against, although it was certainly possible to go some distance down Teoma before turning toward the hills, or even going all the way to Teiri and up its flow. This was more direct. On the far side of A'auwa, about even with the House of

Arierona, we turned onto the path that led over the low hills between his realm and that of the High King and that of Ruapata, further south. The land was lush beyond, farms and forest on either side of our way.

Traders traveled on that road and many of those we walked over the days that followed, as we turned ever to the north and some to the west, passing not so far from the House of the High King at one point. There was no reason nor desire to turn aside to it. We were coming into country I had never seen. Not so Amirea. "This is the way we came when Arierona sent us to the safety of the trade village, when civil war threatened." She looked fondly toward her large husband. "And there Aranu found me."

When he returned from across the mountains with Marareta. Yes, that tale I knew. What, six year ago? Around that. Amirea had been about the age I was now. So had Rahaita.

The land rose and took on the appearance of that around my own home, and then rose more, becoming mostly grassland with the occasional grove of trees. "We are in the realm of Mahutunoa now," Aranu informed me. "The upper reaches of River Teiri are near." He looked about. "I fought battles here, beside your brothers, not so long ago." The great battle where Hara'a's army was thrown back — yes, it happened in this area, and lesser battles that both preceded and followed.

Here Teiri flowed from the east, as it made a great bend further down, before running south to meet the Teoma. Trees lined its banks, willows, wild mulberries, massed green and silver above the water. Open savanna lay beyond them. The river was shallow here and not too broad, and we waded across easily. Our path would angle northwest now to a passage through the hills, the route most used by traders.

With some of those traders we camped along our road. I think they liked traveling with a group of warriors, for there were still a few bands of lawless men in the north, some of them remnants of the rebel force, some of them fighting men who no longer had a master. Not that there was much profit to be had in ambushing those who carried trade goods!

Near dark on the first day north of Teiri, as we settled into our open camp, a small group approached us. Five men only. Said Aranu, "Five only that we see. Be on guard." But outlaw bands were rarely any larger than that and did not attack large groups.

A noble, his warriors — this we could see as they drew close. "I am Ruata," announced the man. "A captain of Momana." Who Momana was Aranu had no idea, nor did Bafa, but I had heard his name in my brother's house. A noble of Mahutunoa's kingdom and one spoken of as a possible successor.

All I knew was that name, that and the fact that he was counted a traditionalist. Nothing more. This noble commander of his had the look of a wrestler, lean and muscular like Hito, but without his proportions, being shorter of limb and longer of body. The face was so ordinary I might have had trouble recalling it a few minutes later.

"Welcome, Ruata," spoke Bafa — being our leader, this fell to him. "You and your men. I am Bafa, son of Arierona." He did not introduce any of the rest of us, remaining cautious.

"The man who seeks stones?" asked our visitor, taking a place in our circle, though his taciturn warriors remained standing at a short distance. We had no fire, eating cold in this land with few trees.

It was hard to say whether there was a trace of mockery in Ruata's voice. "We have heard of you, even here," he continued. "Momana is interested in these metals of yours." I think all there realized at once this was no chance encounter, but all continued to treat it as one.

"Gladly would I discuss them some day with your master," replied Bafa. "For now, we travel beyond the hills and will not turn aside."

"So I shall tell Lord Momana," was the nobleman's polite answer to this. "His lands lie north and east, near the borders of Naire." That was not so close; these men had gone out of their way to find us. Ruata carefully avoided looking at me but I knew his warriors' eyes turned my way from time to time. It made me but a bit uncomfortable and quite a lot curious.

This I confided to Ruiru — and no other — in the morning, when they had departed and we resumed our way. "I too have my suspicions of this man," he said. "All that is to be done is remain watchful." And so we were. A few days later we climbed to the gap in the hills and stood looking northward into the lands of the Diwarna.

It was a bit disappointing that it looked much like the land of the Mora behind us.

36. The House of the Mora

"We are yet far from the valley of the Gurang," Aranu informed us. Only he and Amirea possessed much knowledge of this land. "It is two or three days walk to the trade village, the furthest north that any Mora dwell."

"Officially," Bafa felt necessary to add. We knew there were exiles and outlaws who lived beyond.

I was interested in something else. "I have heard that griffins nest in these hills," I said. I hoped to see one, but not from too close!

"Further west, maybe. They are more likely to fly here from the mountains to hunt across the plains." Aranu looked out over those plains and added, "Only for small antelope and such. Even a lone human is a bit much for most griffins."

"I have heard Ulani's epic about the griffins beyond the mountains," I reminded him.

"Those are larger, and trained by the Lord of the Valley. Even then, they are rarely used to attack men."

No, they fought dragons. Those, too, I would like to see, from yet further away.

More traders followed this road, for almost all crossed through the same pass in the hills. It was a large group that sighted the high roof of the Mora residence in the trade village, three days later. I am sure I could have done it in two, but the laden traders did not walk very fast.

"There are always more of us at the end of the rainy season, when travel becomes easier," one of them told us.

It was so; the village was full of traders, women and men, Mora and Diwarna and not a few that seemed of mixed heritage. The street buzzed like a hive of bees, as they haggled and hawked their goods, invariably in the trade pidgin. "It's practically a fair," said Bafa. This was a word from his language so he must explain it for me.

"Ah, so it is a marketplace?" I thought I understood. "Like maybe on the beach below the Great Falls?"

"Something like that, but not all the time. Once or twice a year." He said then, "Maybe Gordie should make it official."

"He does not yet rule here," was all Aranu had to say about that. Those who did run the village for the Mora, as representatives of the High King, came forth to greet us.

I had never met Ma'are before but I knew the man she had married, Heho, from his days as Hareata's most trusted carrier of messages. He had grown fat! Heho should try walking the roads again for a while, I think. Ma'are was not slim either.

It was she who was in charge here and she who invited us into the House of the Mora, as all referred to it. The warriors and servants too; Ma'are was not one who favored the ancient ways, nor a follower of taboos and 'sacred' practices, nor was this the the Mora homeland. The Taona Marareta had married these two, right here in the trade village, and here they had remained since.

Four children the couple had, the oldest perhaps six, and these were allowed to remain with us as we sat to share a meal. Even among those who were not traditionalists this was unusual. "We want them to be around our people as much as possible," explained

Heho, "so they know their heritage. Only Mora do we speak in this house."

"But of course they have picked up the pidgin outside," added Ma'are.

Heho nodded. "And it is all to the good they have learned it. But we will be happy to return to a land where Mora is spoken not only inside houses!" Heho, it should be noted, had a Kohari father, a prisoner of war who married a Mora woman. This is not uncommon; I knew freedmen of my father who had done so. I think this made him all the more zealous about his Mora heritage.

Inside this house — or on its large and high front porch overlooking the village — was spread a considerable feast. I suppose we took a more or less proper order even if Ma'are disdained tradition, with Bafa and I in the highest places.

"In Gordie's house it is not so," remarked Heho. "Nor are any Mora customs observed."

"We must visit him," I declared. "I will not come this far without going on to see the Gurang."

"He keeps a house here, but mostly to store goods. I am sure he will visit soon," Ma'are said. "And I am sure he will invite you to his — ah, what should I call it, Heho?"

"We might as well just name it the House of Gordie. It is truly a compound such as any in which a powerful Mora noble might dwell." He paused. "Or even a king."

Ma're leaned forward and confided, "I have suggested to him that he should ask to be named a tenth Mora king and bring his, um, domain under the High King. It would benefit all."

This I could not see happening, at least not soon. "Neither Parrots nor Owls would support that," I stated. "Neither would think they had anything to gain over the other." I did not speak so seriously but Aranu nodded; Bafa just sort of gaped at me. Did he not know by now that I was knowledgeable of politics?

"You are becoming as astute as your rival Ma'ave," said Heho. "And almost as cynical." Apparently they kept up on things here too.

Ma'are laughed. "Sometimes people confuse us! We are little alike, my cousin and I." Cousins only by marriage, Ulani had said. This woman had been wed to a relative of Pua's deceased husband, Ma'ave's father.

Heho went on. "My wife is the most modern of modernists. She would sweep away all the traditions."

"We want to free the commoners from the old restrictions. Let them live as they will!"

I was surprised — and amused — that the counter-argument came from her own husband. "In freeing the people from their bonds to their lands and lords, they have been set adrift and have nothing of their own," said Heho.

"A fine one to speak," she countered. "You spent many years adrift, wandering the land as a courier."

"Ah, but in pledged service to my masters. Such pledges hold society together." He took a gulp of his beer. "As you might guess," he went on, "my wife and I have debated this before."

"And he still won't admit he's wrong!" complained Ma'are.

Heho saw there was no more to be said about that and shifted

153

back to more practical politics. "Ma'ave has moved toward the Owls, despite her mother."

"That's her husband's influence," spoke Aranu. We all knew the man she had married, Iro, was of the traditionalist faction.

"I disagree," spoke Ma'are. "I am not sure Ma'ave can be influenced by anyone."

Of this I said nothing, but I thought she was right. If anything, Ma'ave used Iro to further her own political purposes and did not care overly about the issues.

I also thought Heho had some good points. In some places the people were becoming little better than slaves, with no rights to the land they worked. Teme would not solve these problems, at least not until she had a good night's sleep!

37. Trade Goods

Two men went by, carrying what looked like a hammock hanging from the pole that rested across their shoulders. "The best way we've found so far to transport pottery around the village," explained Tala. "A pack-basket still works best to carry it across the hills." The workshop of the half-Diwarna woman and her partner Amlee produced most of that pottery, right here in the village.

Tala also was wife to the noble Mora warrior Taki, whom Gordie wished to take Ma'are's place. It was said that Tala would probably in fact run the trade village. "Gordie has tried to talk us into moving to his house," she continued. "Too far from the markets of the Mora, I think! But Amlee says maybe she could go there and open a second workshop. There is good clay to be found further north."

Aranu whispered to me, "Tala used to be very shy. Her success has changed that." She and Amlee had been among those who crossed the mountains. Why, I will not go into — listen to Ulani's epic sometime.

Gordie was expected. We knew not whether his wife and children would be with him — those were the only reason Amirea had come along. She and Demba had been great friends, once, but saw each other rarely now.

Others of those who came from the sea remained here, I knew. Dutsa, most importantly, who had come to be called Gaho, 'the clever one.' Some called him taona, too, for he was master of those who invented and crafted useful tools. Bafa had gone to him at once and marveled at his 'barrows' and pottery wheels and other devices I did not understand.

I grew bored loitering in his workshop as the two gossiped, and wandered out into the main way through the village. Many were the booths and huts with goods displayed for sale! Here traders from north and south, Diwarna and Mora, met to exchange their wares and carry them back to their own peoples, but some also bought for themselves, those who lived more near. There were woven mats and hides of crocodile and carved wooden bowls and bone fishhooks and whatever else one might need. And, yes, the pots of Amlee and Tala. I followed the way past the House of the Mora and many smaller houses — not all of these were lived in but only served for storage. At the north end lay a small lake, fed by a spring. This was the reason this village was built here in this little bowl-shaped valley.

I should not have walked so far without Ruiru to keep an eye on me. He would be upset. But surely I was safe among all these people! I could see the small stream, narrow enough I might leap across it, that flowed from the far end and knew that its waters ended up in the Gurang. I was ready to follow it at that moment but instead I turned back — to find Ruiru following discreetly behind me. I might have known!

"We may as well go back to Bafa and his friend," I said as I passed him.

He fell in beside me. "There are others from the sea who live here, I hear."

"I think so, two of them. In the area if not the village." I tried to think of their names. They had been at the House of Arierona for a short time when I was still a girl, serving Neatanu — only Dutsa and Gordie had not spent time at A'auwa. When they all came back to this village for safety, when war threatened, two had decided to remain, feeling they fitted better here than among the Mora. And, too, they had found women.

"One we called Digsa, I recall. The other?" I shook my head, unable to think of a name. I remembered he stood out from the rest because of his dark skin, like the Diwarna, almost. The question of what became of Digsa was answered soon, for he was with Bafa and Dutsa when we returned, idly watching them argue over the design of some tool.

"Is this little Miss Teme?" he asked when he saw me. "You have grown tall!" He was an ugly fellow, where one could see his broad, heavy-browed face through his beard. But I liked his smile. "I'm Jack Diggs, my lady. You might remember me some."

"The Mora used to call him Digsa but now it's mostly Aca," said Dutsa, "since no one can pronounce Jack. And it fits him." Aca, in the pidgin, meant 'gather' or something of the sort. "He's a gather-er, for sure, finding what he needs when he needs it."

"Just a trader, Lady Teme," the man muttered, "like a lot of the others 'round here. I do find things for Lady Ma'are sometimes." He looked glum. "Won't be doing that much longer."

"Don't think Tala won't need you," Dutsa assured him. "Me too, for that matter." He hesitated and maybe even an unpleasant thought passed through his mind. "Or Gordie."

My face must have shown I had questions. "Not all of us like what Gordie is doing, Lady Teme," he told me. "Things were fine as they were and, well, I'd as soon have the Mora in charge here."

Aca laughed. "You mean nobody in charge. And I like it that way too. A balance of power, like I heard it called as a schoolboy."

"You went to school?" I could tell Dutsa jested but was not quite sure what he jested about. It did not matter, I suppose.

What did matter was their opinion of Gordie. Of Lord Gordie, I might as well say, for he was certainly a ruler of men. Bafa seemed quite interested in these things as well. After all, he had been named Poneiva's representative, sent to arrange the changes here — or veto them.

"I think," he told me as we strolled back to the House of the Mora, Ruiru close behind, "that our Gordie has probably extended his influence about as far as he is ever going to. There are simply not that many people around here to fill up the land and obey any sort of leaders." He laughed. "And certainly the Diwarna would never fall into line for him."

I do not think the Diwarna even knew what lines were.

By the time we had awakened from siesta, Gordie had arrived, without family but with a retinue of warriors and workers, and the noble Mora Taki whom he wished to take charge here. Hito had told me of him, as had Rahiniti, so I knew what to expect, an extremely large young man, tall, certainly too fat, and a bit inclined to bluster.

"Tala keeps him on the right path these days," Heho whispered to me, "and he knows it."

My eyes went from the imposing Taki to the much smaller

158

Gordie. I had never seen him. He had never been to A'auwa as had most of the others from the sea. Not unlike Bafa was he in size and shape, but paler. A little younger too. A Diwarna apron of woven grass was his only garment. Of this, too, had I been told by Hito, that he dressed as a Diwarna when he was among them — that he considered himself, in a sense, Diwarna, and spoke of them as his people.

Ma'are went out to greet them before her house — hers for now — as we continued to watch, rather lazily, from the porch above. Heho sighed. "I suppose we'll have to get up and put out a meal for him and Taki. Hmm, Tala too, I hope."

I nodded. "She should be here. Women run things better anyway."

"So Ma'are often tells me. Maybe we should get *you* to run this place after we leave."

"I'm sure my brother would order it if I ask," I replied. "But I'll have to go look at the Gurang before making a decision like that.

"Most wise," was Heho's comment. "But let's go see what is to be done here."

38. Things Change

"Henry Wise lives among the Diwarna much of the time now and serves my interests there. His wife is Diwarna." Gordie's own Demba was Diwarna, of course, and the reason he had settled in the north at the first opportunity. "He tried to get the Mora to call him Harry when first he came, which they turned to Hare." This meant 'manly.' "He didn't mind that one bit." A chuckle, shared by others at this meal. "But the Diwarna named him Bamiree, 'golden quartz,' and that is what he uses now."

We spoke Mora, of course. Gordie spoke many languages well, it was said, even the difficult and complex Diwarna tongue. Yes, I know some consider Mora difficult and complex too. The young man — he was but five and twenty Bafa confided to me — returned his attention to the melon in his bowl. He had a piece each of the orange and green sort and was taking bites of them in turn, as if he could not decide which was better. I could have told him the green.

"He is a trader?" asked Bafa.

"In part." Gordie became serious. "He has become a man I depend on to help defend my people there. Kohari raiders have long been a problem on the Gurang."

"One could never organize the Diwarna against them," said Heho and most nodded agreement.

"Things change," replied Gordie. "All things."

"That is why we are here," I commented. It was time somebody brought it up, wasn't it?

"I hope for as little change as possible in this village," Gordie said, "which is why I suggested Taki. He knows how things are done now." The big Mora gave a slight nod in his direction but did not speak.

Gordie continued. "You're supposed to give the approval, right?" he asked Bafa.

"With Aranu's advice," came the answer. I hadn't known this but it made sense. It would have made sense to ask my advice too, but apparently my brother didn't think of that.

Oh, it didn't matter. I would give it anyway.

Gordie looked to Aranu. "You and Amirea are going to visit my home, of course. Demba expects you." He considered his melon slices again. "And any others who wish to come."

"All of us, I expect," answered Bafa. "Even Teme, though her brothers would surely object."

"That's never stopped her in the past," Amirea observed.

I stated, quite emphatically, "I can not return home without seeing the Gurang." This I had said before but it never hurts to repeat things.

Gordie nodded. "Very well. I shall attend to business here in the village tomorrow and we can leave the next day. Taki must have time to be with Tala." The big nobleman and his wife turned their eyes to each other, so I might guess that was where they wanted to be right then. "Taki will return with us, this time."

But maybe not in the future? I doubt any of us missed his implication.

"So how many bodies do we need to fit into canoes?" They spent some time figuring that out, at last deciding to simply bring everyone in our group. Aranu had insisted all his warriors come, and as long as they did, the servants might as well, too.

It would be wrong to suppose we did not speak of the guests when they had departed. "This Taki seems acceptable on the surface," said Aranu, "but the opinion of Ma'are matters most to me. If she thinks he'll do, that will go a long way."

"With both Gordie and Tala to guide him, Taki shouldn't get into too much trouble," was Heho's opinion.

Ma'are said only, "Maybe so. Travel with him a while and form your own opinion. We can speak of Taki again when you return."

I thought that was the end of it until Heho half-mumbled. "I wish Gordie had named Pahe instead."

"Pahe is neither Mora nor noble, Husband," Ma'are reminded him. "He would never have been accepted."

Heho scowled. "Half-Mora like me. It was just his bad luck that his mother was Kohari rather than the other way around."

"But so it is. He is likely now to take Taki's place at his master's side."

So it was, yes. But it did seem unfair. I slept right there on the porch, for the night was dry and warm. Tomorrow, we must prepare to travel again and then — the great valley of the Gurang!

Oh, I know, I was already in that valley. But it didn't look the way the stories had it, around here.

39. Down the Stream

The stream we walked beside was joined by other streams and, at some point, must be called a river. Maybe at the place where it formed a small lake and we took to canoes. It was shallow and sand-bottomed in those upper reaches, and quite clear. Further down it grew brown as it swept into the jungle, its edges disappearing among the shadows of the towering trees. This was more like it — and it wasn't even the Gurang yet.

"We go directly to Lord Gordie's house," said Taki, in whose canoe I had been placed. Of course, Ruiru made sure to board the same one. "Ofttimes he turns aside into the swamps to visit the Diwarna villages there." He swung an arm toward our left; the ground rose higher on the other bank, in places. There I could see the land rose toward the still-distant, pale mountains but that scene was not much different from one glimpsed through a window in my father's house.

For a while it seemed we truly had entered the swamps and only the current told us it was still a river beneath our canoes. "It is like this here and there. Then the banks grow firm again. It is all a great swamp where this stream meets the Gurang, an easy place to get lost." Taki's chuckle sounded something like the mating call of a large crocodile. "I can not find my way through and neither can any Kohari! But Lord Gordie never gets lost. You would think him a born Diwarna."

Taki admired his master, that was obvious. That might not be so good if he were put in charge of the trade village. Some independence would be desirable. And he had good manners, as any well-trained noble warrior might. Not quite the belligerent bully Toare had described to me.

I think life had knocked some of that out of him. Life and Hito, who had once rubbed the big man's face in the dirt!

"The Kohari have never come up here then?" I asked him as we stroked along. We were moving back into an open river now, with higher land on both sides.

"Not yet, my lady, and we'll be ready for them if they ever do." Then the dugouts ahead of us were pulling toward the right bank, and I could see houses rising there.

A dock stood beside a sandy beach with a number of canoes pulled out of the water. We added a number more. "It's yet a half a day of travel down to the Gurang," called out Gordie, waving an arm toward the north. "I'll make sure you see it, Lady Teme!"

The House of Gordie was large, standing on a low rocky rise, and, instead of the usual mat walls, the spaces between the timbers were filled with stones. Around it were many buildings, large and small, a compound to rival that of Arierona, and fields filled with crops, and what must be the beginnings of orchards. Until then I had not realized how important Gordie, this boy-king of the north, had become — had made himself.

But what most caught my eye was not the house and barns with their thatched roofs shining golden in the sun. No, it was right here at the water's edge, the pair of boats tied at Gordie's dock. Like Kohari craft they were, at first look, but no, one could see a little difference here and another there. I wished I knew more of boats!

164

I might have been left there gaping at them while the others went to the house, had not I been noted by Bafa. He came and stood beside me, carefully looking them over from one end to the other. "Gordie is right," he said, not very loudly. He might have even been talking to himself. "Thing do change."

Then to me he said, "I am most certain our host would love to tell us about them. Let's get on up to the house."

The Diwarna woman Amirea was embracing could only be Demba, Gordie's wife. She had a slender, straight body, as many of her people, and dark waves of hair fell on either side of her strong cheekbones. A little girl, perhaps five or so, clung to her skirt.

"Malee," said Amirea to her, "this is Teme." Then she remembered I had never met the child's mother. "Oh, Teme, this is my great friend Demba." Gordie joined us, having discarded his Diwarna apron in favor of a comfortable kilt similar to Demba's.

"Welcome, Lady Teme," said Demba. "I have never met a woman whom the epics named a hero."

Did they know those stories even up here? "Do not forget the Lady Rahaita," I replied.

"Yes, that is so." She nodded thoughtfully. "But there were not yet songs of Rahaita when I knew her. Oorto will wish to speak with you of her. She was almost as much sister to him as I am."

"Let's get inside," urged Gordie. "All of us." Into his great house went we all, his people and ours, nobles, warriors, servants. Inside, it was much like any other Mora house except, of course, it was not Mora. And it was stuffier, maybe, and darker with those solid walls, like being in a cave!

Yes, there were windows. I exaggerated a little. Bards do it all the time so why can't I?

And what were these things? I moved the big piece of wood back and forth, trying to figure it out. "By golly, a door!" exclaimed Bafa. He pushed it so it closed up the entryway and then pulled it back again. So that was what it was for.

"What's wrong with a mat?" I asked.

"I suspect it's here for the same reason as those stone walls," he replied. "Defense."

Oh. That should have been obvious, Teme. We two dawdlers followed the rest in again. "Gordie fears attack," I whispered.

"Maybe," Bafa whispered back. "He's being cautious, for sure."

"It's like the houses of noble Mora in the evil days before the first High King, when each warred on the other. I'm surprised he doesn't have a stockade around it." And suspected one might be to come.

It was late and we were tired, so the meal laid out in the House of Gordie was consumed without any ceremony and only subdued conversation. I saw it was true any sat where they wished at Gordie's meals, even Gordie himself, and men and women mixed rather than each being on opposite sides.

"I will show you around tomorrow," he promised, "and maybe give you a ride in those boats that interested you so." Then he turned to hushed speech with various of his retainers and we heard no more from Gordie that night.

So I found myself with Demba and Amirea, mostly just listening to them chatter. Malee was already abed. I was not really paying attention when I suddenly realized Demba was addressing me. "Aranu is the son of a king," she said, "but the sons of kings do not become kings. This is the way of the Mora and I understand it. But your son might be a king?"

"Not a king but the High King," Amirea told her. "The next will be chosen from a pool of eligible men related to Poneiva by the maternal line."

"Elected by the nine kings of the Mora," I added. "Who are elected in the same way by the high nobles of their realms."

"Ah." She seemed to think on this before going on. "Gordie worries at times about who will succeed him. I tell him he is too young for that!"

Amirea smiled at a thought. "It certainly won't be a nephew or cousin as in the Mora lands. Those all live in another world."

Demba nodded. She possessed more knowledge of such things than either of us, having a mighty shaman for a brother. A mother, too. "Perhaps I shall bear him a son one day and he will follow his father, for we need not follow Mora customs here. Or Malee might be the mother of a line of kings."

There were many possibilities. One was that Gordie's kingdom would not survive him. I would not say that.

40. Lord Gordie's People

"You have the three best archers in the Mora realm here," I informed Gordie. "And four more they taught."

"The few bowmen who serve me are horrendously bad marksmen. I would rather depend on Diwarna with their spear throwers." Of these devices I had heard, but never seen one in use.

Bafa considered this. "Maybe we could design a crossbow. Easier to aim."

What a crossbow was, I did not know, but I could see Gordie take immediate inspiration from the idea. "One would be easier to use in a boat, too, wouldn't it?"

"Ha, Gordie, you are the practical thinker! That's the sort of comment our friend Hito would come up with."

Gordie only smiled. "Indeed. Yet he has become a priest? I expected him to marry some noble widow, as he always said he would."

"He did that too," I informed him.

"The widow of Lord Hareata," added Oorto, who had mostly listened to that point.

"Nothing like aiming high," observed Gordie.

Oorto had been at the House of Gordie when I had risen, seemingly before any others of our party. I had paid little attention to the small Diwarna man seated unobtrusively on the front porch, never having seen Oorto, renowned shaman and Marareta's best friend, before that day.

By the time we were joined by the others, we were friends. Oh, he knew who I was and we spoke long of the lost Rahaita. There had been a special bond between those two, two who had walked together in other worlds.

"Even the great sorcerer beyond the mountains, Hurasu, who taught both of us, was shaken when he felt her death," Oorto told me. He could speak with this man in some way — I knew this but did not understand it. "He told me that even Pana'a sensed his emotions. She did hot know how to communicate with him. Hurasu could have tried to send the prophetess a dream but saw no purpose." He shrugged.

"You know she says the son of Marareta will be as you. He will need training."

"As will the daughter of my sister and Gordie," he told me, and laughed. "I know this task falls to me."

Malee too? Oorto would be busy! What was he doing? The Diwarna had suddenly sat erect, eyes unfocused. So he was for far longer than made me comfortable. I was ready to run inside and find someone, when he relaxed and — returned.

"That was my master," he explained in a calm, low voice, "asking after things here. Also he told me that he felt another death beside your sacred lake, one who had some power but was untrained."

"Hoka," I whispered.

"He did not know the name but he had touched the man before." By then, others were bustling about in the house, and wandering out onto the porch. We rose and entered.

So it was we now followed Gordie about his compound, arguing about bows and crop rotation and many other things. "Kalina," I observed, as we passed one field. "To smoke or make ropes?"

"I would prefer the latter," replied our host, "but my people insist on some for their pipes. I may try planting tobacco too, one of these days, but it is not a need right now."

"Your people, Gordie?" asked Bafa. "Just how many is that?"

"I haven't counted! I like to consider the Diwarna mine, but I do not command them. Many who come to me are of mixed birth, people who can find no place in either Mora or Diwarna society. Here, that does not matter.

"There is a valley up that way," he said, swinging an arm toward the southeast, "where more of mixed blood have settled, and displaced people of all sorts. Marareta found that refuge as he returned over the mountains."

I had heard mention of it though it was not spoken of in any epic. "We have a sort of an alliance — no, make that an understanding — and men and women from there come and go in my service. I also see it as a place where my people could retreat to safety, were it found necessary."

"Gordie himself could slip into the swamps as readily as any Diwarna," said Oorto.

"Lord Gordie calls it an understanding," spoke the lean taciturn warrior who had accompanied us all the morning. "But they have come to see him as a leader." This was the Pahe mentioned by Heho, a man whose mother had been a Kohari slave and father a Mora trader. We do not look so different, we and the Kohari, and he could readily have passed as another Mora commoner, had he chosen, enlisted as a warrior somewhere, maybe even married well.

Instead he named himself Pahe, 'bitter' in the Kohari tongue, and chose to serve Gordie. "That is up to them," said Gordie, and led us on.

When we returned to the house for a midday meal, the discussion inevitably turned to metals. "I found copper nuggets where Hito directed me," spoke Gordie. "A truly good source remains undiscovered. I haven't time to explore across the Gurang."

"I don't suppose you've seen any tin," Bafa said.

A laugh. "I wouldn't know it if I saw it!"

Bafa drew forth a pouch and shook out a couple of colorless, rather lackluster gems. "This is what Hito called 'star stones,'" he said, "but it is also tin ore. The Kohari sometimes use it for jewelry and that is where I have been obtaining it. Keep one for reference." He put the other back. "I can't find a source for it either."

"So let's go looking in the morning," suggested Gordie. "We can take my new boats down to the Gurang and I'll show you some of the river and some of the places we've found copper. Gold, too, but that isn't so useful!"

"Like Bafa's silver," I said. I had remembered the name he had given it.

"Silver, eh? You'll have to figure out how to make mirrors with it. They would be a marvelous trade item!"

"And even more dangerous than bronze weapons," observed Bafa.

41. The Great Gurang

Aranu was torn between going with us or remaining — that is, whether to protect me or his wife. We managed to convince him I would be safe enough with Bafa and Ruiru to keep an eye on me. Still, he insisted that half our warriors accompany those of Gordie, and Bafa thought this was a good idea.

I knew Kohari boats. Not well, but I had seen them on the beaches below the Great Falls. "These are not sewn together, are they?" I asked Gordie as we boarded. The Kohari used palm fiber to join the boards and then coated them with some resin to keep out the water.

It was Pahe who answered, and who seemed to be Gordie's Second on this expedition. Taki had been left behind, in charge of the house. I think he knew nothing of boats, and two men of ordinary size could take his place!

"We have a better way, my lady," he answered. "Our boats have bones!" He pointed to something but I did not understand his meaning.

"A framework inside to hold everything in place," Gordie explained. "Pegs to connect the boards to it." Ah, I saw this.

"That is clever," I admitted.

Gordie laughed. "Our people have built boats in this manner for hundreds of years," claimed Bafa, speaking to us from the adjoining boat. "Amirea's father tried to teach the Mora but old Temani'itu would rather have had bigger canoes."

"We came to your land in such a boat," added Gordie. "It rotted away on the beach by the falls, I hear."

The lines were released and we floated out into the stream. "This doesn't look much like it though," commented Bafa. "More like a Chinese junk."

"You'll think so even more if we put up a sail. I wanted something with a shallow draft to navigate these streams." Gordie looked over his little fleet, the two large boats and five canoes, also of good size. "Ho, Pahe," he called to the man, who was busy with the lines. "I'll take the other boat." With that, he nimbly stepped up onto the rail and over to the adjoining vessel. Now he and Bafa could gossip all the way to the Gurang.

I wished Oorto had come along but he would rather be with his old friends at the house. This I certainly understood. I would have to make do with Ruiru and Pahe for now.

As with Kohari boats, we had oars, not paddles. I would not be denied the right to pull with the others. Would I not be paddling were we in a canoe? Was I some old woman, no longer able to do her part?

I admit it took me a while to figure out how not to entangle myself in the other oars!

Soon, we were again in swamp and all semblance of a river disappeared. Even the current was difficult to follow, sometimes seeming to flow all directions at once. And the trees — never had I seen ones of such height. "Are these the sort we use for our great canoes?" I asked. I knew the largest were shaped of logs from the Gurang.

"Those come from further down," came an answer from a fellow rower. "It's too far to float these big cypress."

"But we use them for our own canoes," said another. "And for the boards of these boats."

"Yes, none of that flimsy kuru wood the Kohari use," the first added. So many things to learn!

Such as how large a river can be. I found out soon, as we rowed out of the swamp and into the Gurang. One could hardly see all the way across; I wouldn't want to try to swim it. Especially were it full of man-eating crocodiles, as the stories told us.

And as both Gordie and Pahe warned all of us who were new to the river. "Do not put your arm or leg in," growled Pahe. "Not all of it may come back."

We put up our sails now, rather clumsy square ones. No, not quite square, a bit longer on one side than the other. Sticks ran through the mats from which they were made, side to side, to stiffen them. Up Gurang we went, against the powerful flow. I did see the monstrous crocodiles sunning themselves on the banks and shivered to think one might be swimming just below me.

It was mid-afternoon when we pulled over to those banks, at what looked a much-used camping site, with a sort of cove where the canoes could be pulled out. "Our base of operations," announced Gordie. "We'll use the canoes to explore along the shores tomorrow." He turned to his guests and warned once again, "Do not get too close to the water!"

I stayed very far away. I thought to place my sleeping mat further up the shore than any of the others — let the crocodiles eat them first! — but Pahe dryly informed me, "There are leopards and bears in the forest. Best sleep closer to us, my lady."

It was pleasant there, none the less. The night air was hot and humid, admittedly, and there were biting insects, but we had a great fire in our camp, and many strong warriors around it. Some sang and some told jokes I did not understand. In the pidgin, of course, which probably explained it.

"We've decided on two days," Bafa told me in the morning. "Or three nights, if you prefer. Then a day back." He tilted his head and looked at me. "Do you want to ride around in a canoe today, looking at rocks, or stay here? Many of the men will remain in camp."

I decided to stay, at least for the morning. Ruiru, naturally, remained with me. I amused myself shooting arrows at things for a while, and even hit some of them. Whether they were good to eat, I was uncertain but intended to find out. Then I napped.

Too long I napped. It was well into late afternoon and some canoes had returned by the time I woke. I would go with them tomorrow, I decided. Flocks of parrots passed overhead, headed to their roosts, and ibis, some white, some bluish, but all tinged pink by the sun falling into the western sky. Something very large flew so high above us I could barely keep my eye trained on it. A condor? A griffin? Who could tell? It disappeared toward the mountains.

The men were exceedingly careful in the beaching of their canoes, even in the relative safety of our cove, for they knew a crocodile could suddenly burst from the depths and take one of them. Some would stand with spears, keeping an eye on the dark brown water. I thanked the gods we had only small, fish-eating crocodiles in the rivers of home.

Stones. Some shiny, some dull, some too large to hold in my hand, others like grains of millet. Bafa and Gordie picked over them, picked them up, put them down, all the evening. They were not yet done when I fell asleep.

42. Gathering Rocks

"I think Pahe and Ruiru may have, ah, hit it off," whispered Bafa. Gordie glanced in their direction and shrugged.

"Wasn't Pahe Oorto's lover?" I whispered in turn. Hito had mentioned it.

"Not for some time," said Gordie. "Too many things pulled them different directions." He looked toward the pair again and asked, sounding more a playful boy than a ruler of men, "Should we have you ride in Pahe's canoe so Ruiru can be with him?"

"Ruiru needs to pay attention to Teme," said Bafa, not jesting at all. "I'll go with Pahe today."

Up and down Gurang we went, mostly along the far northern side, where the banks were often high and rocky. "It is likely that copper nuggets could be found up many of these little streams," Gordie told me, pointing out one that fell into Gurang from about the height of a standing man. "Little has ever been explored over here. Even the Diwarna don't come across much."

It was at a place like this Hito had fallen into the river, or so he had described it to me. I wondered if there were water dragons around, such as aided him. "I've been taking note of them all and will eventually try to explore up some of them. Or send men to do it."

"There are good places to defend here," remarked Ruiru.

"If there were anything worth defending. And it's all too open to the river." I could see Gordie's point. A house here would be a target for raiders who came up the Gurang.

Ruiru responded simply, "If you find your stones you will have something to defend."

That too, was a good point. But Gordie had not found his stones. "Here," he said, and picked a greenish pebble from the rocks beside our canoe. He rubbed a bit of the surface away and I could see the gleam of copper, 'sun stone' as the Korhari name it.

"You have a good eye," I told him.

He looked up at the low cliff. "Who could guess where this came from? It might have fallen from right up there or washed many leagues down the Gurang." Gordie sighed. "There is a huge treasury out there, in the unknown hills and mountains. Not just metals that might someday be useful but the quartz and flint and obsidian we use right now. We might do better to search for those."

He looked to the sky. "And now we search no more. Let's strike for the camp." Five we were in that canoe, all paddling, and we reached it soon.

Bafa had picked up a good bit of gold during his day. "I know, it's not much practical use, but I would like to experiment with it back home."

"Maybe you could make a calf or two," Gordie told him, and his tone seemed sarcastic. I had no idea what he meant. Bafa explained to me much later, quite patiently, that he was making fun of the gods and maybe of us. Gordie did not believe in gods of any sort! That seemed very strange but did not bother me much. The gods can take care of themselves and so can I.

That evening, Gordie told us as we sat by fire, "We came down to Gurang mostly so you could get a look at it." He nodded in the general direction of Bafa and me. "I didn't expect to find much, though one never knows. The men picked up some copper, and some pretty and useless jewels. We'll head back in the morning and you can stay in my house as long as you want.

"Oh, he added," speaking directly to me, "Demba would gladly have your friend Rahiniti come back to visit. She almost talked the girl into staying and living with us the last time."

This had never been mentioned to me, not by Rahiniti, not by Hito, who had accompanied her. I must ask them of it on my return.

I lay awake some that night, listening to the sounds of the jungle behind us, the cough of some great cat, the calls of the night parrots, a bellow that might have been anything — and definitely nothing I would wish to encounter in the dark. Would I ever hear such again? I had seen the Gurang once; perhaps that was enough wandering for Teme. Perhaps it was time she married someone on the shores of A'auwa.

Just who that would be, I was quite unsure.

Somewhere around noon the next day, we turned to our left, into what looked like the same swamp we were already passing and that which lay ahead. Gordie's river, I did not doubt at all. Was there a name for it? I had heard none and had taken to naming it Gordie's River in my mind. We had made good time, with both sail and current aiding us. Now there would be rowing against the flow. But this river was sluggish compared to the Gurang; there should be no difficulty finding a sleeping mat in the House of Gordie tonight.

179

ARROWS OF HEAVEN

Three canoes paddled ahead of our boats, which traveled side by side, and two behind. Only those behind could I see, for we faced rearward when rowing. A voice rose behind me, and more, men calling from one vessel to another. I craned my head around and there, in the middle of the river before us — for we were exiting the swamps — floated three Kohari boats, filled with warriors.

43. Two Battles

Yes, three boats they were, slightly larger than ours. Three clumsy Kohari boats, with warriors near equal in number to our own. Gordie's voice rose above all else. "Find your weapons. None can return to tell of the way to my house!"

Some would have to keep rowing and paddling, of course, but I would not be one of them. "Archers!" Bafa called, maybe even louder than Gordie. "Find your marks!"

'Archers' meant Bafa and myself and two bowmen who had accompanied us in the boats. The other two had remained behind at the house. I knew we would be the most valuable warriors Gordie had, at least until the boats came together and men could fight hand to hand. I knew also there would be archers among those Kohari.

I would have called out the same orders had not Bafa, in the other boat, been slightly quicker. That did not matter. Two archers in each vessel. That was ideal. "Get us on either side so we can shoot at them," I cried. To whom, I know not; maneuvering the boat was someone else's job. A few wobbly Kohari arrows came our way. Those did not worry me much — the men in the canoes would be in more danger from them. We needed to keep them from being shot before they could get close enough to board.

One arrow after another I released, carefully, at least half hitting their mark. I have no doubt the other archers did as well, or nearly enough so not to matter. Ruiru was surely having a fit with me standing where I could be made a target. Then the boats and canoes were all together in the middle of this brown river, men leaping from one to another, as we drifted downstream, no one longer at oar or paddle.

There was little I could do now. I am no warrior, to swing club or ax against an enemy. Nor do I intend to ever take part in another battle. I am only a girl with good aim!

I retreated to the far end of the boat and watched Gordie's men cut down the invaders, the fight turning to rout, some Kohari attempting to escape into the water. We archers did not need to bring ourselves to shoot at those swimmers. I saw the great green-black bodies of the crocodiles roll as they took them under.

The victory seemed almost too easy and we soon realized why. Many of these men had already been wounded in some other battle. Some there were in the bottoms of the boats too hurt to fight. Gordie shook his head, ordered their throats cut, and sent their bodies toward Gurang. We were no longer moving that direction, for some were back at the paddles now.

"Should we take the boats, sir?" called Pahe. Gordie gave him a distracted nod. He was surely thinking of where these Kohari might have already fought and the likely answer was his own house. The three boats were towed behind three canoes, paddled by the fewest men possible; the rest of us left those behind as we rushed upriver.

Save those who did not survive the encounter. Three of our men lay dead. Our men? Gordie's, I should say. Others were wounded.

"We might not have won here were it not for you and your archers," said the man beside me as we pulled at the oars. "I have heard men name you hero and I now believe it."

"And she took charge at once," said another. "Not only brave but a leader."

Those thoughts of living peacefully by A'auwa came back all the stronger. It is one thing to be named a hero in epics but another to live it!

There was a column of thin smoke rising ahead. "That is nearly burnt out, I would say," came Pahe's voice, calling from the other boat.

"Those not rowing, ready with weapons!" barked out Gordie. No need; we could see as we approached that whatever battle was fought here had ended. The canoes by the dock were all smashed. The raiders might have attempted something of the same with the dock itself but there was little actual damage to it.

The smoke? It rose from the burnt-out remnants of a couple of storage sheds near the river. The House of Gordie stood undamaged, and before it stood Taki and Aranu, apparently directing cleanup. Taki still held a huge stone ax, no longer needed as a weapon, but used to point here and there.

Aranu motioned to him to stay as he hurried down to report. He gave us a look and immediately realized we had been in battle too. "You caught them as they ran from us, I take it."

"It is so," answered Pahe, "but they will run no further. How much damage?" He asked these things, for Gordie was already running toward his house.

"Little. We were ready before they came ashore, for the Diwarna had seen these Kohari on the river and the man Bamiree had time to warn us, and to fight beside us. The alarm was sounded and we met them before the house. Taki is a great fighter! I would have him beside me in any battle."

Pahe smiled grimly. "Still, I will be glad to see him in the trade village and myself in his position. But that matters not right now. Were any warriors slain?"

"Four." Aranu grew serious. "May they feast with the gods. Good men you have here, Pahe." He was briefly silent, perhaps from respect. "Bamiree too. Or Hare, as my people would name him, and name him well. He returned to the swamps when the fight was done."

I could see Gordie returning, more slowly. All must be well with Demba and the others. He stopped a moment and talked with Taki before continuing to us.

"Those in the house are safe," he said, to no one in particular. Maybe I should go on up there. "It is to be hoped," Gordie continued, "these Kohari blundered their way here rather than being guided. Either way, I need to build more fortifications. What one raider can do, more will." He turned to me. "I understand your archers were as useful here as on the river."

"Bafa's archers," I told him.

"If you will. I am also told that Amirea came out on my porch and loosed shafts as well." Now that I would never have expected. But we all do what is needed, when it is needed, no?

44. A Coming Together

"I will not return to the village with you," said Gordie. "I intend to keep myself well away from the decision you make."

Bafa nodded. "Understood. I must say that Aranu highly recommends Taki now. However, being a great warrior is not the sort of qualification I'm looking for."

I must insert my view into this. "But he's honorable. That counts for much, doesn't it?"

"It helps," Bafa allowed.

"And he's obstinate," added Gordie. "A little too obstinate to be my Second here, honestly. I suppose I should send him with you."

"If I name him to the post, he should probably be there," was Bafa's laconic reply.

"Oorto is coming too," I reported. "He told me so this morning."

"Then probably Demba knows it, as well," said Gordie. "I should get back to my project. A farewell feast tonight!"

The 'project' was two low stone walls being constructed between his house and the river. I had guessed wrong about a stockade but not too far wrong. Bafa and I walked up to the House of Gordie.

"Those battles changed everything here," he said, not very loudly. "You recognize that, don't you?"

"People can see he truly is a power up here now, able to defeat the Kohari rather than hide from them. I'm not sure he believed it himself."

Bafa sat himself down on the front steps rather than climbing to the house. "Gordie has done what Nesmith — Nezama, you called him — had intended. Made himself a king. It is something with which his neighbors will have to deal."

I laughed. "I don't think he is ready to challenge my brother yet!"

He laughed with me, but after a moment's introspection, said, "By the time the next High King is chosen, Gordie's opinion might matter. Or whoever succeeds him."

We sat there a while, watching workmen pulling stone-laden sleds. They should have some of Dutsa's barrows here, I thought. As the sun sank, we went in and prepared for the farewell feast at the House of Gordie.

It was hard to say goodbye but I was ready to live among the Mora again. In the morning, we began the journey, first to the trade village, then home. For the most part, we were in good shape. There had been no serious injury to any of us, nobles, warriors, servants, in the recent battles. With us came only Taki and Oorto, first in canoe, then on foot.

"I go only this far, to the village," said Oorto, as we rounded a low hill and saw it spread before us, the House of the Mora rising above all else. "But I shall come to the land of the Mora soon. It is time I visited the house of my friend Marareta and looked on his son."

I wondered what would happen if — no, when — he encountered Ulani. The two had last seen each other at the House of Revaru, five years ago, and I had been told it was awkward. Oorto had never traveled further into the Mora realm than that house. There would be much for him to see.

Now, there were things to see for a last time here in the trade village. It was perhaps slightly less busy than on our departure, but only slightly. There were still many traders with their goods, and much noise, and we were surprised to see several Mora warriors wandering among the stalls. Who would bring fighting men here?

That was answered at the House of the Mora. The man who sat with Ma'ave in her gathering chamber we did not know, but I recognized the one beside him. Ruata it was, the noble who had visited us on the other side of the hills. Was this his lord, Momana? That would explain the warriors.

Such a high noble visiting this village was unknown. "Lord Momana," spoke Ma'are as we entered, "I present Lady Teme and Lord Bafa." We were the highest ranking Mora in our group, so it was for us to introduce the rest of them. Then we sat and I looked at this Momana.

He was a tall man but not so tall as his cousin Mahutunoa, who is one of the tallest Mora I have ever seen. Or tallest of any men, since I know none taller than the Mora. Momana was neither young nor old, but did have the look of a hardened warrior about him.

I was puzzled that the man was not eating, although many varieties of food had been laid out for us as soon as we arrived. But he did converse with us.

"I camped here a couple days ago," he told us. "It was time to see what was on the other side of the hills. I recognize that this area grows more important and is on my own borders."

Bafa said, "But you must go roundabout to get here, through the pass the traders use."

"This is true," the nobleman admitted. "There are many places one may cross the hills but that gap is the easiest way, and the one best located for trade between this place and the Mora realm. We have a pass that is not too bad on the edge of my lands. It opens to nowhere, too far east to be very useful."

"The hills are higher over there," observed Aranu. "More a spur of the mountains."

"Still, it would be good to know more of that pass," Bafa said, obviously curious. His great weakness — or strength. Who can say? "Were I not going directly to the House of the High King, I might have asked to see it."

"Anytime, my friend," spoke Momana. "You would be welcome as a guest. And perhaps we could discuss those stones of yours. I have many questions!" He laughed rather loudly. "And many stones!"

The nobleman did not linger, leaving us to our meal, but promised to speak with us on the morrow, when we had rested. Aranu's first words on his departure were, "I like not how he looked at Teme."

"I noted that too," admitted Bafa. "He has a wife, does he not?"

"Two of them." Ma'are said that. "An ambitious man such as he might well desire a third, if she is sister to the High King."

I did not like that idea at all. "He hopes to succeed Mahutunoa, right?"

"Yes," she replied, "but he is not that much younger than the king, and Mahutunoa has a knack for surviving." There were laughs all around at that. "Mahutunoa has a deserved reputation for caution," Ma'are went on. "It kept him alive and in power through the recent wars."

Yes, Mahutunoa was a prudent leader, who knew when to retreat so he might fight later – not quite a typical Mora warrior mentality. He was also somewhat of a moderate, politically, though recent events had pushed him toward the Parrots. I would suspect Momana did not like that.

"He is not staying with you?" I asked. It had seemed strange he would leave the house to eat and sleep in camp. A high noble would expect to be accommodated, normally.

Heho answered me. "He refuses to stay at our house, or eat here, as he disapproves of how Ma'are and I live." It was rather obvious that Heho likewise disapproved of Momana. "He is one of those very strict traditionalists who feels he will be —" He searched for the right word. "Polluted by our ways."

Ma'are but smiled at her husband's vehemence. "Lord Momana does not disapprove of the nontraditional work of Dutsa. He has spent time at his workshop, asking many questions."

Heho snickered. "I do not think he understood the answers."

Bafa looked down the line of men seated to his right. "I have something to say to the noble Taki anyone might understand." The big man looked up from his food, perhaps slightly confused. I do not think he had been paying much attention. "As representative of the High King Poneiva, I approve of your appointment here. Now run and give Tala the news!

"And you," he said, turning to Ma'are and Heho, "had better start packing. We return in two days."

Both smiled. "We began weeks ago," Ma'are told him.

45. The Road Home

"I would that this Lord Gordie had come with you. We should speak, he and I."

"He should come in a few days, Lord Momana, if you can wait."

This seemed to present a difficult decision for him, for he furrowed his heavy brow in consideration. "Nay, I had best return to my lands. Some other time." Then, as a seeming afterthought, "Or he would always be welcome in my house."

Ma'are spoke with the nobleman but Taki was at her side. In two days, such things would be his responsibility. "Perhaps," she said, putting as little into the word as possible. We all knew it would never happen. Even Momana, probably.

"I have no other business here, then," Momana went on. "I and my men will start on our way, hmm, at noon today." He turned to Ruata, who hovered near. "See they are ready."

"Yes, my lord," he near-whispered and slipped away. His voice was almost as bland as his face.

"It was worth the trip anyway," said Momana. "I needed to see this place. And it was good to be here when a new man took charge of it." He nodded rather respectfully toward Taki. These two were of nearly the same height, certainly the two tallest for several days walk any direction!

"So I say farewell to you all, noble friends." He turned and walked from us with no further ceremony.

Taki watched him go. "He asked me many strange questions," he said. "About whether Lord Gordie sought allies and whether he was going to arm his men with weapons of metal. I would not have told him even if I knew."

"He is feeling things out, wondering whether he can influence what goes on here," was Oorto's opinion. I had not seen much of him since we arrived but he apparently had kept an eye on us. "You know not to trust this man so I shall not warn you."

"He'll be gone shortly," said Bafa, "and his dozen warriors with him. I'll speak to Poneiva of him when we reach his house and then think no more of him. And you," he went on, turning to Taki, "be sure to report all this to Gordie."

The big man nodded. He probably intended to but it was good to remind him.

Two dawns later, we were prepared to follow Momana from the village, all we who came here weeks earlier, and Ma'are and Heho and their children and a pair of their servants. With a large group of traders traveling south would we journey, at least at first.

"I shall see you all soon, it is hoped," spoke Oorto in farewell. "Perhaps, Teme, I shall finally behold the A'auwa you and Marareta so love." He turned to Ruiru. "And maybe another I love."

Was I confused? This was not at all what I thought had happened at the House of Gordie! "I thought you and Pahe —" I started to say to Ruiru.

"Pahe loves only his master," he said. "There is no room in him for more."

"I, too, learned that," spoke Oorto. "Who knows if we shall meet again, Ruiru, but I shall look for you by A'auwa if I journey there."

"And I shall be there, at the new shrine of Wenatu I have vowed to build," answered Ruiru. The two embraced and that was that.

We walked south, toward the pass through the hills, and home.

Part IV. The Target Struck

46. In the Night

I had barely fallen asleep. It seemed I couldn't breathe. For a moment I dreamed that a crocodile had me, was dragging me under the dark waters. Then I woke and realized there was a hand across my mouth, and more gripping my arms.

There was no way to cry out. They were dragging me away, away from my sleeping friends. Was there no sentry? A glimpse of a prone body told me what had happened to him.

I struggled. No use; these were strong men. Three of them? One shoved a piece of bark-cloth into my mouth and they rushed me away, carrying more than dragging now, my feet barely touching the ground. "Bind her," I heard someone say and knew there were more men there now. And that even voice commanding them — surely that was Ruata.

They tied my hands behind me, but not my feet. We were going to travel on, I guessed. The cloth between my teeth was readjusted and another piece wrapped around my head so I might not spit it out. "This won't be necessary for long, my lady," came the low voice of one of my captors. Ha, even in kidnapping they would be polite to a noble lady!

"To the pass?" asked one.

"No. East we go," came again the leader's voice. I was even more sure it belonged to Ruata now. "We'll go by the high gap." There were some sounds of displeasure over this but no objections.

If Ruata led these men then Momana must have given them the order to take me. I could see no other explanation. So he had been behind it; I should have spoken more loudly of my suspicions — and Ruiru's.

It was so that they felt safe removing my gag by dawn. I could see they were five including the leader who was, indeed, Ruata. The same warriors with whom he had visited our camp once, I thought; they must be his most trusted men.

"Do you take me to Momana?" I demanded to know. "He should know what my brother will do to him!"

"Lord Momana has taken the familiar path of the traders and would be across the hills now, openly traveling east to his house. Who would accuse him of anything?" asked Ruata.

"But my people would know he was behind this."

He shrugged. "They would suspect it. That is not the same thing. And it will be known that he was in the realm of Mahutunoa when you, ah, disappeared."

They would know I was gone by now, and possibly hours earlier. Someone would surely be tracking my captors. Aranu? Ruiru, for certain.

We traveled on, quickly, through the day, the hills growing ever closer on our right. We were angling toward them, sometimes running, sometimes walking, but steadily moving to the southeast. The hills were higher here, I could see, and scrubby thickets filled the shallow valleys that ran toward them. There seemed to be a well-marked path for us to follow. Who traversed this country? And why?

A brief camp, some cold dried meat, an hour or two of sleep, and we were on our feet again. So it went for days. Four? I am no longer sure; my mind could hold no thoughts by the time we turned into the hills themselves. Up through winding rocky ways I was led. Momana did not lie when he said it not as easy a path as the one the traders took!

I do remember wondering if I would see a griffin at last.

But I saw only vultures and curious marmots. The actual pass was not so bad, broad and easy to walk, but that climb to it would discourage any laden traders. And it was an easy enough way on the far side, descending toward the Mora lands, though not so gently as further west. We did not descend all the way.

A turn to our left, a path that clung to the hillsides, and then left again into a narrow cleft. "Should we blindfold her?" asked someone.

"Late for that," said another. "We should have done it before we turned this way."

"No need," came Ruata's voice. "Lady Teme may know all our secrets."

Further into the dark crevice we advanced and suddenly I realized it was no longer a crevice at all, as it opened into a great room with a high-vaulted ceiling, a light filtering from somewhere above. We had entered a cave.

47. Momana's Cavern

I do not like caves. Nasty things live in them, bats and large insects and even bears. This one, I will admit, was not so bad, nor even damp as are many. And — "Men made this, didn't they?" I asked. It looked too regular.

Ruata gave me an approving look. "In part. Slaves added to what was here naturally."

"You mean took away!" said one of the warriors.

Another laughed at this and said, "They added space." The men were settling down on the floor, able to rest at last, it seemed.

"I travel with a band of philosophers," stated Ruata, sitting down as well. "Rest, my lady. We'll have a real meal shortly."

I sat on the floor. There were no mats that I could see. "There are others here?"

"A pair of trusted slaves. Trusted because they are blind and can not find their way out." He leaned back, reclining, his eyes on the cave roof above us. "You will want to know why you were brought here. That is not for me to tell so you might as well not bother asking."

"I am sure I shall learn in time," I replied.

"You are wise, my lady." There was little in his tone for me to read. "And too good for Momana, I am sure. That is no matter for me."

I assumed the nobleman would come here eventually. And as I had said, I would learn in time. The two servants, man and woman, and neither young, had entered the room. Blind, as Ruata had said?

Yes, they did not look quite in our direction as they addressed us, asking if we wished food. I hoped that was natural and not done to them when they were brought here.

While they hurried away — rather quickly, considering they could not see where they went — to fetch a meal, I thought on things. My mind was growing clearer as I rested, at last. Food and sleep would help even more. Momana was going to act as if he knew nothing of me and go to his own house. How long would he stay, pretending, before he came here or had me sent there?

I can not tell you for it was hard to keep track of days in Momana's cavern. Yes, the light came from outside somewhere, through some opening in the rocks above, so one could tell day from night. But I was tired and slept much at first, so I don't know how many changes from light to dark I might have missed.

It all depended on how cautious or impetuous the nobleman might be, how soon he wished to put whatever scheme he had into motion. Would he use me against my brother somehow? Propose marriage? Ask me to train his archers? How was I to know?

But come he did, and rather soon. I think he decided to see me before any men sent by my brother arrived at his house. Were we far from that house? There was so much I did not know!

He strode in and addressed me as if nothing unusual had happened, as if I were simply a guest. "I can not stay long, my lady. I expect visitors at the House of Momana!"

I could guess who those might be. Immediately I asked, "Do you think you can make my brother do your bidding?"

"No, I intend to make you my bride." He sounded quite sincere, like a suitor sure of his cause. "Then the High King will be my brother and my friend."

This I had feared. And expected, to be honest, as the most likely explanation. Momana was hoping to help his chances to succeed Mahutunoa by taking the sister of the High King as wife. And maybe, too, produce a son who could be the next High King.

"And if I refuse?"

"You are a woman," he said, "and should learn to obey. Also, I shall be a king. What man could offer you more than that?"

Names came to my mind. I was a bit surprised by which came first. "Perhaps you are right, my lord," I murmured. No sense in upsetting him, I felt, at least not right now. I also felt that Momana had not thought all this through very well, but simply fixed his mind on an idea and pursued it. Couldn't the more sensible Ruata have dissuaded him?

And if he was sensible, maybe I could promise him rewards from Poneiva if he got me out of here. This I might try when Lord Momana was gone.

Ruata entered the room, if one can call it that — we were in the large space I had first seen on entering. There were a number of other chambers and tunnels, I now knew. He came close to Momana, speaking lowly as the tall noble leaned down to listen. "Bring him," he said, and turned back to me. "We shall have another guest, my lady," Moamana told me.

Ruata returned, two of his trusted warriors following, and between them, a prisoner. Blindfolded was that captive, his head wound in bark-cloth, but I could see it was Bafa.

48. *Two Prisoners*

"I have no time to speak with you right now, Lord Bafa," said Momana, "but many things to say when I do." He turned to me. "And to you as well, Lady Teme." He abruptly left the room, just as he had entered it.

In the mean time, they had unwrapped poor Bafa's head. "Teme! Just the girl I came to rescue."

"I've been waiting for you," I told him.

"This one and his friends tracked us here," said Ruata. "We were surprised to see them climbing toward the pass." Bafa gave the man an unfriendly look. I could guess there had been a fight. "It does not matter. They could never find this place and now they have no leader." He whistled loudly, which I had learned was the signal for the slaves to come.

"Food for our guests," he told them, and laughed. "We have two now."

The guards — who did not guard very closely but loitered by the only entry — paid us no mind as we ate and talked. "Ruiru and I followed the trail, with four of Aranu's warriors. He took the rest of the party on toward the gap but sent one man running ahead as a messenger to your brother." He chewed a bit on some dried papaya. "I suspect messengers are rushing all over the place now."

"No doubt. But no one knows of this place nor is there any evidence Momana was involved."

He considered this. "I wonder why he wanted me as a prisoner."

"Maybe he wants to marry you too," I told him. Then, quite a bit more seriously, I asked, "Were any of your men killed?"

Bafa shook his head. "I do not know. I sort of got grabbed right at the start and didn't see what happened."

"An ambush?"

"Pretty much. I hope Ruiru's alright. He'll keep looking for you if he is." I knew this was so. "This is quite a place," he went on, looking about the cave.

"There is much more of it," I said. "I suspect there is another way out but I don't have any chances to look."

"No, I wouldn't think our hosts would approve of exploration. Their pass should be explored, too. Not useful for trade, I think, but an army might want to use it someday." He smiled. "Going which direction, I can not guess. And, well, I noticed other interesting things on the way up to it."

I could make various guesses about those but did not feel like it. "I'd be more interested in knowing just where we were."

He shrugged. "Somewhere in the northeast corner of Mahutunoa's kingdom. Maybe near the border with Naire."

"Where Momana rules." That I knew.

"And no one bothers him much, it being a poor land, and remote." Bafa might have left it at that, and I thought he had, when he added, "He has certainly found a good way to attract attention now."

"Maybe that is what he wants," I mused. We would not figure Momana out; better to turn to what we might do here.

It seemed when we walked through the caves — where allowed — Bafa was more interested in the rock walls than what lay between them. He examined the shimmering translucent columns that hung from roof to floor, the color of pale night-blooming flowers. He looked up much, into the shadowed vaults. Wondering if it were possible to reach a way out? I would not think it so.

But he whispered to me, "If any of my men live, they would know we must be near and set a watch. We may be able to do no more than wait for what will be."

"Who was capable enough to follow our trail? Not you, I am sure!"

"One of Aranu's men. I asked for the best tracker before we left camp. Maybe he can pick up mine now." I remembered the rocky ground we had crossed and felt no more hopeful than Bafa sounded.

So we waited for rescue or Momana, whichever came first! Of Ruata we saw no more, for he undoubtedly served his master somewhere rather than being wasted on us. His four taciturn — and philosophical — men were in and out. At least one, I noted, bore wounds from the encounter with Bafa's party. I much doubted they had slain them all. Or any.

Our guards did not care where we might sleep, so Bafa and I moved our mats into one of the smaller cave-rooms, one with a roughly evened floor, and light from a slit in the roof, far above. We could glimpse a bit of blue through that opening, unreachable but perhaps giving us some hope. Sometimes a stray swift flitted down from it — we could hear those nesting up there somewhere. No bats, I thanked whatever gods might be listening!

A sound awoke me. Something had fallen from above; not so unusual, for the bird droppings and refuse came down regularly. That, we were willing to put up with for the sake of the sun's light. Again. I sat up and looked about the dim room. It must be near dawn, and most of the light still came from the stone oil lamp burning near the entry.

A bird call? It sounded like no swift, nor any other I could recognize. "Bafa," I called lightly. As he roused, I went over to stand beneath our 'sky light,' as he named it.

Looking up, I saw Ruiru, looking down!

49. Getting Out

Bafa walked over, took a look, and gave him a cheerful wave. "I hope he brought a very long rope," he whispered. I doubted it. I doubted such a rope existed anywhere within many leagues of us, and could certainly not see a lone man dragging such a length up the hills.

Our visitor disappeared after waving back. Nothing else could he do right now, but surely Ruiru would bring back men to rescue us. Oh, who knows? He might even find a rope! We were certainly ready for rescue of any sort.

The gods must have decided to play a jest on us for Momana returned that day, Ruata at his side. "Your friends have gone home," the towering nobleman reported. "Or at least are no longer at my house."

Ruata muttered, "Your cousin allows them to camp near our border, my lord."

"Yes, yes, I know. And he has moved toward us, as well. It is of no matter." I could guess his man did not agree, but his bland, round face revealed little. "Come, Lord Bafa, I would speak of things with you." He gave me a glance, as if I hardly mattered. "You may sit with us if you wish, my lady."

That, perhaps more than anything Momana had yet said or done, made me wish to sight down an arrow toward him. As if I were unimportant, an afterthought! But I would not miss their talk, so I followed after without speaking.

"The man Aranu is quite stubborn," Momana continued. "He

would have used his ax on me if others had not dissuaded him."

Aranu, eh? He must have headed this direction as soon as he got our party across the hills. Others surely followed after him.

"He is the son of a king, Lord Momana," came Bafa's even reply. Then, with a little more flint in his voice, he said, "We are accustomed to having our way."

I was astonished at how quickly the nobleman's anger came. For a moment I thought he might strike Bafa! "Here, I have my way," he spat out. Then, just as quickly, his rage left him. Bafa appeared to take no notice of any of this.

It reminded me of when he had questioned Momana's henchman before Arierona. Bafa was in control and the nobleman did not even realize it. We sat down to a small meal spread on mats, in a chamber beside the main large one. Beyond was the kitchen where the blind slaves worked and slept.

For a couple minutes, we but ate. It was the freshest food I had seen or tasted for several days, probably brought along by Momana and whatever retinue accompanied him. "I want to have a workshop here," he announced after a while. "Like the one of Taona Gaho in the trade village, or the one I hear you have at Arierona's house."

Bafa considered this and asked, "To make what, my lord?"

"Weapons! I would know the secret of your magic metals, Lord Bafa, and arm my warriors with this bronze. We could be a great nation here in the north then. We could ally ourselves with Lord Gordie and rule all the way to the Gurang!"

This was, anyone but Momana would know, the most crazy of

crazy schemes. Who had encouraged him in such thoughts?

Bafa nibbled on a berry, seemingly in thought. "An ambitious plan, Lord Momana. The difficulty is not so much in making my, um, magic metals but in finding them. So far, not nearly enough has been discovered to equip even five men with weapons."

"This is so?" Momana turned to Ruata, the anger of before returned. "Why did not I know this?"

"My lord," he began, cautiously. "We told you the noble Bafa traveled in search of his stones." It was dangerous to contradict a man like Momana, and Ruata surely knew this. Mayhap it was not the first time it had been necessary.

"Hmm, that is so." Momana nodded. "Yes, it is so, Ruata. Accept my apology." He turned back to us, all anger forgotten. "Then we shall find them here. I told you we had many stones!" Momana laughed quite uproariously and went back to his meal.

He spoke of unimportant things after that, asking after gossip in the great houses, of relatives I had never met, and such things. At the end, he told Bafa, "I must return to my house and you must remain here." He pondered a brief moment. "I can not yet allow you out to find the proper stones. Later!"

Then, to me he said, "You return to my house with me. Ready yourself." And off he went to some business he had elsewhere in his caverns.

"This complicates things if Ruiru comes with help," whispered Bafa. But there was nothing to be done about it.

Momana, when he returned, had only a couple attendants with him, a pair of veteran warriors. Had he brought only these from his house? "Come," he ordered. There was no blindfold nor were there bonds. Could I break away maybe? Now that Ruiru had found us, that might not be the best idea. It would not do for me to lose myself in these hills.

Still, if the opportunity presented itself — I would see. Out into the crevice in the rocks we went, the way I had come in. "Why do none know of those caverns, Lord Momana?" I asked. They must be far older than he.

"Others began to shape them before you or I were born, my lady, perhaps even before there were Mora in this land. Who could know?" He walked before me, and did not turn his face my way, so I could see no expression. But his speech was that of ordinary conversation, not a man in the midst of kidnapping a noblewoman. "The caves were discovered in the days of my father and their secret kept carefully, so they might be a refuge if ever we needed one."

And he had needed one, but perhaps not for the reason his father had envisioned.

50. The House of Momana

The rest of Momana's warriors were camped somewhat below, in one of the many hollows in the hills. It would be reasonable to assume they did not know the way to the caves. And, as I had guessed, the House of Momana was not so distant from those caves — half a day's travel, if one hurried. These men hurried.

It did not seem a particularly impressive house, when it rose before us, neither large nor tall. But new; that I could see, the timbers certainly no more than four or five years cut. Even some scent of pine yet lingered. Momana himself must have chosen to build here, closer to his hideaway and the pass through the hills, rather than live in an ancestral house.

His men closed about me as we approached, to prevent any from spying. But would news not get out, once I was in that house? Ah, we went not to it but a smaller building some distance behind, beside a garden turning brown at this season. Little grew about Momana's house, in truth, where it sat on a rolling terrain of grassland, a lone tree standing here and there.

Most Mora nobles lived close to the commoners they ruled over, the women and men who tended the fields, who served in myriad ways. And the nobles served them, in turn. So it should be, I think, with obligations both ways. Momana was choosing to live separate from his people.

Into the smaller house I was taken, and left there under guard, as Momana returned to his home. Were his wives here? Did they know of me? Ah, ask not questions you can not answer, Teme.

Rather, see if there is any way out!

In most Mora houses, made with walls of grass or palm mats hanging between the timbers, it is no great problem to force a way to the outside. At least this was so further south, in the houses I knew. Here there was a lattice of stout bamboo wands. Thickets of such bamboo I had seen in the hills. Maybe I could get through, with effort and time. It was unlikely I would have the latter.

Momana should be cautious about showing me yet but sooner or later he would go through with his plan of marriage. He must know my brother, my friends, would not stop watching him. Poneiva might just come in with a troop — with or without the permission of Mahutunoa — and search the compound.

And Ruiru knew of me, and of Bafa. On him, more than any other, must I trust.

Momana visited me around dusk, accompanying a slave bringing food. I could glimpse Ruata outside. "I am told that Naire has now come to our border," he announced. "As if that weakling could do anything!" Naire's kingdom lay east of Mahutunoa's, the furthest east and north of any Mora nation. There mad Hara'a had ruled before him.

"Better than his predecessor, my lord," I murmured. This man had been on the right side in the war, I knew.

"Oh, certainly. Hara'a was insane, and obsessed —" He stopped suddenly, remembering just who I was. "But you know all about that, of his pursuit of Rahaita and of his death." Yes, since I was the one who slew him.

"I know you are something more than most women. More than

210

most men, maybe! That is one reason I desire you as a wife." Momana focused his gaze on me, a gaze almost menacing in its intensity. "But remember, my lady, unlike Hara'a I have no obsession. You are a means, not an end."

Momana did not always sound stupid. Often, but not always. "And therefor valuable," I countered.

His mood changed at once. "That is so!" he laughed. "It is good that you understand things, Teme. We can be powerful together."

That was true. I could make this man important, as he wished, guide him to kingship, give him an heir who would rule as High King. None of these things did I desire. So I only nodded and smiled on the fool. He soon left but I could see he was full of plans.

That was a night I slept in captivity, in what I guessed was a storage shed. Close, it was, stifling even, but not too warm. We were up higher here; I had not noticed that in his caves where the air always seemed to feel much the same.

It was Ruata who came in the morning, along with my meal. He gave me a long, impassive look. At last, he spoke. "Momana has made a foolhardy decision to marry you at once, thinking this will protect him."

Was this my chance. "You know this is wrong, Noble Ruata," I said. "My brother will reward you if you help me get away from here."

"Undoubtedly," was his only reply. I could make nothing of that.

51. Out and In

So I should make a break for it. Ruata did not seem inclined to aid me, not that I could tell anything for sure with him.

Indeed, he was right in implying that it would not protect Momana to marry me. As soon as I had Poneiva here — and he would definitely demand to see me once the marriage was made known — I could divorce him and the man would be — what, executed? No, exiled, maybe, disgraced, certainly, and never to be a king.

But I would rather not go through a marriage ceremony with Momana and certainly would not want to go to his sleeping mat after. No, not for even one night. Not that it would kill me if it happened and I could still divorce him at the first opportunity.

That all figured out in my head, I began to plan an escape. Tonight I would work my way through one of the walls. I had already weakened some of the fastenings — sapa root, they looked to be — and not hurt my fingers too much in the doing of it!

I would have given much for a good flint knife. First, I ate well; there was no reason not to. I knew the bowls would remain until the morning. At least that was how it had gone with last night's meal. I would not expect any intrusion.

I would also have given much for an oil lamp. The bindings must be loosened in the dark. I thought if I could undo three of them I could force my way through, at the corner of one of the bamboo panels. It must be done quietly!

Perhaps it was midnight by the time I slipped out, felt my feet touch the ground outside the house. The bamboo scraped my back as I worried my body through. As far as the guards went, I must trust on luck and the gods; two sat outside the entry and every now and again one would make a circuit of my cage.

I suspected those checks came less frequently as night wore on. I stood in the shadow of the wall now, a shadow only slightly darker than the night. Which way? There was little shelter about Momana's compound, no place to conceal myself. I would be spotted readily, come day, if I tried to run across the open fields but I had some hours until then. Maybe with enough head start.

No, go the other way, toward the hills. They would never expect that, and there were more places to hide. I ran from the shelter of one building to another standing beside the garden. A mistake — there were dogs in that little house, penned up. I remembered when Toare had expressed his disgust about the idea of eating them and at once realized that these were being kept for just that purpose.

Not that it mattered. A yapping dog is a yapping dog and this was very many yapping dogs! And I was spotted. It did no good to run, though I tried. Soon I was in the house of Momana, my hands bound, and thrust into a sleeping chamber, with a guard at the entry. I wondered if Momana had even been awakened.

He did come in the morning, gave me a quick look, and remarked, "We will wed tomorrow. Then you will obey your husband and there will be no more foolishness." I saw no more of him that day. If only I would not see him on the next, either!

Ruata himself brought me bowls of food later. "I think you can feed yourself without unbinding your hands, my lady," he said. He crouched and watched me eat for a while, not speaking.

At last, he said. "You will not wed Momana, my lady. Of that have no fear."

"You will turn from his service?" I knew this was the most difficult of decisions for any warrior, to repudiate the lord he followed.

He turned his bland, inscrutable face toward me and said, his voice low but even, "I do not serve Momana but another. We have used the fool for our purposes and now it suits those purposes that you die and Momana be disgraced." He shook his head. "I tell you this so you may prepare."

Oh, it made sense! Another had been encouraging Momana in these witless decisions, and Ruata a part of it. "So it must be," he finished, and left.

But he would return, would he not? And then — a knife? Strangled? I wondered why he had even told me. Was it the same sort of game he played with Momana, laughing at those he controlled, powerless against him? Or maybe he truly meant it as a kindness. It made no difference to my fate.

I must attempt another escape. I knew not how. It would be possible to get through the flimsy grass-mat wall, maybe, if the guard didn't look my way for a while. But I would still be bound and in the house of Momana. The guard — no, he was one of Ruata's trusted few. It would do no good to ask him to go to Momana for me.

Ha, now I was hoping for aid from the man who had kidnapped me! It must have been at the time many napped, early afternoon, when a figure appeared at the entry, spoke a few words to the guard, and entered. Could this be the end?

No, it was another, someone quite unexpected. "Lady Ma'ave?" I whispered, for it was surely my cousin in all her tall and somewhat wide self.

She knelt down close and whispered, "Momana and my idiot husband think I have come to talk sense to you. I did not expect to find this when I came to his house, believe me, Teme!"

Ma'ave slipped something into my hand. A stone blade!

"I would almost rather use it to cut your throat," she said, but her voice did not sound too serious. "How could Iro let himself become involved in this?"

It was fortunate that he had or Ma'ave might not have been here. I knew it was not for me she did this — well, maybe in part, for Ma'ave was not evil, only ambitious — but to save her husband's reputation and, most of all, so I would not be married to Momana and bear him a son. That would be the last thing she would want!

She could not have known that Ruata — and whomever he served — had other plans for me.

"Now I am taking Iro and departing this place! We will not be involved in anything Momana had planned nor be anywhere near if your brother comes. But," she continued, "I shall most certainly let him know you are here, if you do not manage to escape." And with that, Lady Ma'ave rose and left me, and not slowly.

52. Out Again

I shall always be grateful to my cousin, rivals though we are, and to whatever gods whispered in her ear.

It was not difficult to turn so the guard could not see — he rarely looked in my direction anyway — and saw through the bonds on my wrists. What then? I could probably cut quickly through the wall and be gone. How soon it would be noticed, who could guess?

But there were several mats rolled up in here, and rolls of the bark-cloth. The room had served as storage before I was thrust into it. Quietly, carefully, quickly, I arrayed some of these on my sleeping mat, covering all with piece of cloth. It took but a few seconds, I know, but felt like I worked much longer! If the guard did not look closely at the shape in the shadowed corner, he might think it me. Then I sliced through the wall with one long cut and slipped into the next room. Which also was used as storage, and unlit, thank Wenatu!

I threw a cloak of bark-cloth around me — many did so in the cool of the evenings so it would not seem strange — and stepped into the hallway. Not that way, that would take me to Momana's central gathering room. His great porch was over there, then. The way to my right would be best.

This time, straight away and into the fields, I decided, as I emerged from an entrance near some of the outbuildings. Would that I had more weapon than a single blade of quartz! I went slowly, casually, as if I had every right and reason to be strolling through Momana's compound. The open entry to one of the little storehouses caught my eye. Was it luck? Was it the gods? I know not, but a jumble of weapons could be seen in the rear.

Perhaps it would have been wiser to pass, to not dawdle so close to the house, but I could not resist. There was a bow, in the Kohari style to be sure, but it would serve. And short enough to conceal under my cloak! Arrows? Yes, a quiver-full. Probably warped and badly fletched, I told myself, but I grinned with the joy of this discovery.

Then I was beyond any structures and striking out across the open hills. The rest of that day and through the night I traveled, walking, running, resting only when I absolutely must. West, I traveled, as that was the most likely direction to find friends.

One who was not a friend guessed this. Not long after dawn I saw men behind me, distant. They must have found me missing far too soon! And then, Momana's men would know the country better, the quickest paths to travel. I could only hurry on, hope to stay ahead.

This was mostly open rolling land — I have said this before — and the hills were of good size. A few small trees grew here and there and by the occasional narrow stream that rushed down from the higher hills beyond, heading, ultimately, to Teoma. Those streams, small as they were, had dug deep gullies I must cross, gullies tangled with brush.

My pursuers were gaining. As things were going, they would catch me before I might hide in the night. I was most incensed that those men were outrunning, outlasting, me, Teme! That was surely Ruata himself leading them. Four in all, unless others had flanked me without showing themselves. That is something I might have tried in their place.

If I had the men for it, of course. I suspected these were the only ones who came this direction. It must have been well past noon when I decided to run no more and halted atop one of the tall grass-covered hills, where I could see anyone approach. I had my bow; I would use it.

The first arrow flew high. They looked at it a moment and came on, all the faster, incautious. The fools should have known I only tested the bow and the wind with that arrow. I drew the string back again, smoothly, as if aiming at a straw round beside A'auwa, and let another arrow fly. Ruata fell with it through his throat.

I frowned. I had aimed for his chest! Another arrow was already nocked, ready for me to draw back and release. My pursuers had stopped and, moreover, thrown themselves flat on the ground. No fools were they! But they did not advance; it seemed they were arguing what course to take.

Their leader was dead. I had no doubt of that. Still, they might hope to take me back to Momana or maybe the unknown man Ruata served. They might simply seek to kill me, for many reasons, including revenge. Or they might see no point in going further.

Then they were sliding forward, on their stomachs, presenting poor targets for me. I might use up all my arrows and still not stop them. Better to run again. I turned to see more men rushing toward me, past me, to attack those who pursued. Bafa! Ruiru! They had taken their time but rescued me at last.

The battle was short. Unprepared and outnumbered, lightly

218

armed, worn from running all the night and day, the men of Ruata were cut down, none offering to surrender. So it ended, for then.

But who had been Ruata's unnamed master? Would that ever be known?

53. Laying Plans

It was Ruiru who spoke. "I and the others had wandered about, searching for some sign of you, when we noted a wisp of smoke rising from the rocks. Your captors were not careful, it seems, about hiding their fires."

"They surely believed none would ever see their smoke, there in those forsaken hills," observed Bafa.

"So we found some of the holes that let smoke out of and light into those caves. I heard your voices at one and waited till dawn to make myself known to you."

"And hurried off to find help?" I asked.

"It seemed the best plan. The help we found was most unexpected."

"Taki," said Bafa. "Rushed along our trail with a band as soon as the news came to him. Didn't even stop to ask Gordie!"

"He had Oorto to help him track us. All Diwarna are good trackers."

Bafa added, "But Oorto is better."

Ruiru nodded agreeably. "We considered trying to come in from the top but we remained patient and the entry was eventually revealed. Men must come and go from those caves, at times."

"And then in they popped and delivered me from two sentries and a pair of blind servants." Both laughed.

"So where do we go now?" I asked. "After I sleep for a long time, I mean."

"Our messenger is on the way west," Ruiru reported. They had sent a man at once. "Mahutunoa and whoever is with him will know you are safe, and your brother soon after."

"And now they know for certain Momana held me, they will come here into his lands. Poneiva would never let this go unpunished." I was absolutely certain of this.

Both also seemed to think it likely. "We might as well wait, then," said Bafa. "I say we go back to Taki at the caves right now. It's not far."

So we decided, and I did not even rest that long. By noon the next day we were at the cleft that hid the entrance to Momana's cavern. Perhaps Momana's no longer. Only a handful of men were there and Taki not among them.

"Some went off to scout east or south of Momana's house, thinking you might go one of those directions, or that they might come upon someone with information," reported Bafa. "I do not know where Taki has disappeared to."

That was soon answered. "Our sentries told of men approaching from the other side of the hills," said one of those left as a guard. "He went to see this."

Before dark, we knew their identity. Gordie accompanied Taki into the cavern, and several warriors with them. "A useful hiding hole," remarked Gordie, looking about. "But that pass might be even more useful."

"In more ways than he thinks," Bafa whispered to me. What secret was he keeping?

Gordie continued. "I suppose I couldn't take possession here, even though it tempts me. Too far away."

"And in the lands of the Mora," I pointed out.

"That might be argued. The hills are empty of men so who can say who owns them?"

Bafa laughed. "You are ambitious, my friend!" Gordie did no more than smile and spoke no more of such ideas.

He did say, however, "Now I am here, but not really needed. I did hurry, Lady Teme! Perhaps we should go visit this Momana." Gordie gave us a slight and not at all mirthful smile. "I have a good body of warriors waiting just on the other side of the hills."

"Better to let the Mora handle it," said Bafa. "Leave things to her brothers."

Gordie nodded, seeming to agree. It was the sensible thing. But I must speak to them of other things, those things I had learned in the House of Momana. As we ate there in that cavern, I laid out all Ruata had told me of an invisible hand.

Others joined us during the night, I found on rising, those men who had been out searching for me and now returned. Oorto was among them, seeking any tracks that might have been left had I flown to the south. He sat in the main chamber, where many slept now, seemingly in thought.

The Diwarna looked up as I entered. "Greetings, Teme. It is good to see you are safe." I took a seat beside him. "Gordie has gone to his men on the other side of the pass, to wait if needed." A knowing smile. "I think he will keep men there from now on and make that path one he controls."

"Then my brother should do the same on this side. Or Mahutunoa."

"Or Naire," added Bafa, who had come up noiselessly behind us. "It might be argued which king has ownership. There is no clear border." He chuckled as he took a seat. "Nor has there been a need for one before."

"That question I am willing to leave to your people." Oorto sighed, so slightly it could have been no more than an exhalation. "When Gordie returns, I shall ask him to give my farewells to my sister. I had hoped to do it in person, before coming to the land of the Mora. But here I am."

54. Many Came

"Many came rushing when they heard," stated Revaru.

My brother Beka smiled indulgently at the youthful king. "Needed or not!"

If Revaru did not worship both my brothers, he might have taken offense. Instead he let loose a good-natured laugh. "I think Teme never needs any help!"

"I need all of you," I told them, and knew it to be the truth.

And indeed many had rushed here. It surprised me. We camped just within what was recognized as Momana's western border; not a great force, not an army, but a decent raiding party. On learning I was safe, Mahutunoa had withdrawn with his men, saying he would leave the High King's brother to see to the High King's sister, and deal as he would with her abductor.

Mahatunoa was once again being prudent.

"This one insisted on coming with me from Poneiva's house, leaving his master behind," said Beka, indicating Toare, who stood with his band, a spear in hand. Hadn't he been told he should stick to a club?

I may have been touched but I snickered anyway. "The boy can't decide whether he is bard or warrior."

"Whichever you need at the moment, Teme," was his eminently sensible answer.

"And Revaru joined us on the way with his handful. Your personal guard, aren't they?" he asked the young ruler.

Revaru nodded. "Do we march to the House of Momana?"

"We wait on Aranu," came Beka's answer. The noble commander had been sent to scout with some of his men, to see if Momana was gathering his own warriors, if he was even remaining in his house.

Also to deliver a message to Momana, telling him to surrender himself to the judgment of Poneiva. It was a dangerous undertaking, delivering such a message, the sort that got messengers killed.

Beka motioned for me to go aside with him, before muttering, "We met the Lady Ma'ave, hurrying with her husband and entourage toward the High King's house. She told us things."

"I am grateful to my cousin," I stated. "I might be dead without her aid."

"And so I am sure Poneiva will overlook her presence in Momana's house or anything in which she might have been involved. Her husband's, too." He chuckled and confided, even lower, "She informs me she intends to divorce Iro at the first opportunity."

"Maybe find a husband she can control more easily," I replied.

"I wish we had been aware of this other unknown man before I spoke to Ma'ave. She might have some idea about him."

I could only shrug. "Perhaps. Ma'ave could have glimpsed someone who came and went at that house, thinking nothing of it." So might another, I realized. "Or Iro. He was closer to Momana's plots." I almost wished I had been there longer so I could have learned something.

Aranu arrived with a report that some welcomed and some did not. Revaru, always spoiling for a fight, certainly approved.

"He will not surrender himself," he told Beka. "Momana, I

think, prefers to fight and die a heroic death, rather than come before judgment. Heroic in his mind — he lost all honor when he took Lady Teme."

Beka shook his head. "My brother would not have executed him. At worst he might have stripped him of power and possessions and sent him to live in another kingdom. Comfortably, even."

Beka might have been surprised but I was not. Live as a guarded guest in some other man's house? Momana thought too highly of himself for that.

Aranu had more to say. "King Naire has brought a small force west. He will join us if you allow it."

Bafa leaned in to offer advice. I was thankful he did, for he had a better head for such things. "He would be useful to prevent any warrior of Momana coming to join him from further south. His old house, the one of his predecessors, lies there, and more of his men." I am not sure how Bafa even knew this.

But I definitely agreed with his idea. So did Beka. "We'll send a messenger asking this." He raise his voice so those around might hear. "And then we march in the morning."

55. A Challenge

There was to be no battle. This somewhat improved my opinion of Momana, as he chose not to throw his men away in a hopeless cause. He was still stupid, of course.

One man came from his house and announced, "The Noble Momana asks for single combat against a champion. Then no others need die in battle."

"And if he wins?" asked Beka. I doubted the middle-aged Momana could defeat the best we might send against him, but there was always that possibility. He was a big man and an experienced warrior.

"Then you may send another." Thus we knew Momana intended to die that day.

"This does not need to be," was all Beka said, and sent the man back to his master. None of us expected Momana to be dissuaded from his chosen fate.

"Who shall it be?" asked my brother. "I will not claim this as my right." Though he could.

"All those who wish to face him should throw lots," was Aranu's answer. The nods of those standing about showed that most approved. It would have to be nobles only, though I am sure many a warrior of common birth would have liked to fight Momana — Ruiru surely included.

"I will," spoke Revaru, first and most eager, as ever.

"And I, of course," came from Beka, and then Aranu and Toare announced that they must be included. Finally, Bafa shrugged and added his name. It was not necessary, I thought, and wished he had not. He was good enough with weapons, and had fought beside Beka and Marareta in the civil wars — the three 'heroes from the sea.' But he was not the equal of the others.

Now all Mora are great gamblers so there were many dice ready at hand. "The high cast wins," announced Beka, and each threw onto a mat spread between them. I think I held my breath. "Six has Revaru. He is our champion."

"I wish Taki were here, rather than in the hills," I whispered to Bafa. I am not sure which of us chose to stand by the other. "It would be interesting to see him against Momana."

"Revaru will do well." His laugh seemed to hover between relief and regret. "Better than me!" I could only agree with that, not that I would say so.

But I did say to Revaru that he was surely the best and the gods had chosen him for this. I looked on the young king, handsome and powerful, and knew why I loved him, once.

Then came forth Momana. He had the full armament of a noble warrior, and even an attendant to bear his spare weapons. A small shield protected his left, but he wore no armor, no crocodile hide breast plate as many might. Nor did he have a helmet; only his high ceremonial feather crown, green and gold, rose from his head. A short, heavy spear was in the right hand. Ah, it would be so easy to put an arrow in him from here and end this.

So Revaru likewise chose to wear no armor, foolish chivalrous boy that he was, and went forth armed in the same manner. He issued a challenge, raising his spear, but I could not make out the words from where I stood. I half-wished I did not stand there at all, that I was not watching brave Revaru fight this man.

The fight was joined, jabbing with spears, not throwing. Momana's size was not the asset it might have been when he was younger. This I could see. He was slow on his feet. But the long and still powerful arms were as quick as ever. Revaru used his spear more as a fighting stick, striking out with the shaft rather than the point. So had I seen men fight before.

So had I seen Hara'a fight Marareta and nearly slay him. Revaru, as good a warrior as he was, did not match the dead king's skill. Both backed off following minutes of inconclusive attack and parry, and Momana cast his spear aside, holding out a hand to his attendant. The man gave him a war-club.

This seemed fine with Revaru, who dropped his spear as well. He chose a heavy stone hammer in its stead. Now club and hammer are used in very different ways; one slashes and jabs with the club of hard, flattened wood whereas the hammer is for striking blows. This Revaru could do very well. I had watched him at it.

But the Taona Marareta considers the war-club to be the king of all weapons, in the hands of a skilled warrior. It was ever his own choice, as it is my brother Poneiva's. He still practiced with the bronze club Marareta had made beyond the mountains.

And Momana's long arm should give him an advantage with this weapon. Ah, but not his slow feet. He could not turn quickly enough to follow up on his thrusts, and Revaru ducked away, attempting to connect with great whistling swings of his hammer. Then, our champion — maybe I could even call him my champion

229

— changed his attack and swung low, catching Momana on the leg. I knew all would be over in a few seconds.

Limping as best he might, Momana returned to his own attack but stumbled forward into another wide-swung blow. Down he went and did not rise. Nor could he with brains and feathers spread across the grass.

May some god or another receive Momana. I had no love of the man but he had died well.

56. The Three

Naire arrived before dark. I had seen the man, once, when he visited Poneiva. Naire was not a young man, and seemed unusually unassuming for one of the Mora's nine kings. This was a position he had never expected to hold, being elected after the death of Hara'a, as a leader offensive to no one.

He joined us as Momana was laid in a grave. The nobleman's servants had dug it, on his order, before ever he came out to meet us. Of Momana's widows I saw nothing. They must have remained at his other house through all of this.

"So ends this," spoke Naire, to all of us, or maybe none of us. "But not the troubles of the Mora."

It was Bafa who responded. "You see more challenges to the High King, sir?"

The king's voice was gentle, but not his words. "I do. Poneiva is generally well-liked by the nobles so there is no great unrest among them. Among the commoners, this is not true. The High King is remote enough from most that his rule means nothing to them." He paused a moment, watching dirt being shoveled into the grave. "Those who are dissatisfied will find leaders, or leaders will find them."

"You sound like old Temani'itu," Beka said. "You must come south so we can hear your voice more often."

"Others can fill that role better than I," was his reply. "Younger men." No more did Naire say of this, nor did he even mention politics again before marching away with his men the next morn.

There was little reason for us to linger long either. Momana's successor would be chosen by others and was Mahutunoa's concern, as whoever ruled here was his vassal. Naught had been done, nor even mentioned, about the caves and the pass beyond them. This, too, was perhaps best left to Mahutunoa, and maybe Naire — both had been informed of what was up there. Oh, no doubt Gordie would seek some say in that now, with his warriors at the other end of that path across the hills.

Not enough warriors to make an impact on the Mora kingdoms. Gordie did not have that much wealth and power, not yet. But enough to make his voice heard.

Bafa gazed in that direction as we discussed our trip home, as if desiring to visit the hills again. A messenger had been sent to those there, to Gordie or Taki or whoever still lingered. Then he shrugged and turned his face west. "Back to your brother's house, I guess."

"You can return to searching now for your metals," said Toare, who seemed to keep close to me, whenever he could. As did Revaru, I had noted. And the two recognized each other as rivals, oh yes.

"No need, my boy. I found a lovely vein of copper in those hills where I was held captive. Saw it as I was climbing toward the pass."

Ah. So that was it. "But you still need the other stone," I reminded him. "Tin." I was a little proud to have remembered that.

"I am sure there are deposits on the Salt Coast. We'll find them if we keep looking."

"You thought it best not to tell Gordie of this," I realized, of a sudden.

"So it is," he replied, and chuckled in a rather self-satisfied manner.

And so we would travel to the House of the High King, our intended destination when we had left the trade village. How long ago? I was not sure of the day at all! I should ask someone — when it mattered again.

Yes, I and these three men — little more than boys, even Bafa — whom I had loved, at some time, and considered possible husbands, also at some time. I knew now which I truly did love. But he must realize that he loved me, too, mustn't he?

Heroic Revaru, tempestuous, impetuous. One I had both loved and battled. Sweet Toare, solid as any man might be but with his poet's soul. Bafa, he I had near worshiped as a girl, an archer, seeker, thinker. Any one of them would have done — as I said, at some time.

We could have gone roundabout to my brother Poneiva, to the House of Mahutunoa and then that of Revaru, taken our time, been feasted. I would not have minded, I will admit! But Beka wished to hurry home, maybe to prove to our brother I was yet in one piece. Southwest we angled, not always even finding roads. Savanna gave way to forest and farm fields, and wider streams for us to cross. None too wide to wade or swim; we would not take the time to search out canoes for our crossings.

"This looks more like home," remarked Revaru. We might well have been in his kingdom at the time, so that is not surprising. We would not turn aside to his house but I wondered if Revaru would.

A morning came when we camped by a winding, tree-shadowed river, the calls of a hundred sorts of birds greeting the dawn, and he said, "It is time I go to my home, Teme." He put his arms about me. "I know there is another here you love, not me. May the gods bless you both."

He was right. Revaru and his men went one way that morning, we another. Ah, I did love that brave, bulky, thick-headed boy of a king, but not enough to marry him!

Two days later we were walking the wide and much traveled dirt road that led by the House of the High King. Another day and we spied its high roof and saw Poneiva coming to greet us.

57. A Talkative Man

"We actually caught another would-be assassin lurking about," admitted Poneiva. "As the other we captured, he knew nothing of value about anyone higher up." He shrugged. "He might not have even had anything to do with the others."

"Have you had a conversation yet with Lady Ma'ave?" asked Beka. It was the three of us only, the siblings from the south who now lived in the House of the High King.

"I did, and she was genuinely apologetic that she knew so little. And quite genuinely angry at her husband. Ex-husband now, isn't he?"

"Soon," I said. "He's the one to talk to." Ma'ave might have been as angry about being left out of the loop as anything else.

"He shouldn't be hard to squeeze," was Beka's opinion.

Poneiva nodded an agreement. "We'll have to send Bafa home soon, and Aranu and Amirea. I'll miss having their little girls here."

"Don't hurry," I told him. "Ruiru is going to leave your service and head to A'auwa too, isn't he?"

"He has promised to accompany you back if you go soon. But yes, he will serve another now. First Hito and now Ruiru. We lose many good men to the gods!"

"I think he and Oorto will stop first at the House of Marareta," said Beka.

"That will work out as it works out," I told him. "I suppose Ulani and Toare will be on a path to somewhere else too."

Poneiva stopped walking, and stood there looking at me. The

four guards who followed at a discreet distance as we meandered through the garden must also halt. "Do you intend to marry that boy?"

I grinned at him. "Should I?" He made a disgusted noise and walked on. Beka, however, gave me a knowing look.

It was not allowed for me to question Iro. Why, I do not know. I would have done a good job of it. But I was allowed to observe. Most important, Poneiva took my suggestion that Bafa take the lead.

"Momana had friends among the traditionalists, we know," began Bafa, as if conversing with an old friend. "You among them, Lord Iro." The man only nodded. "But, of course, your views are moderate and you support our High King."

"That is so, Lord Bafa," he allowed. Iro was becoming more at ease. He was a fat little man, who always seemed about to say something important and never did. Iro leaned toward Bafa, saying, "I think there were those more extreme among his friends. Strange men came and went."

"Did he introduce them?"

"Um, no," admitted Ma'ave's husband. Yes, still, and I think she had convinced him to be open with us. "But I recognized some. Leaders of the more, um, extreme sort in the north. And — and —"

"Yes?" asked Bafa, as if he were only mildly interested in the answer.

"Agents of some higher up nobles down in this part of the nation. Not just our party, either."

"Such as?"

"Ikataki. Never the man himself, you understand." He became surer of himself, once he had let that fact out. "But some of the messengers certainly came from him. Yes, certainly." He nodded his head vigorously.

Now Ikataki — as you would know if you have been paying attention to me — was a leader among the Parrots, the modernists, and a cousin of ours with eyes on the dais of the High King. Indeed, were my brother Poneiva to meet mishap, he and Mouiri would be the leading candidates.

"We thank you for helping us with all this, Lord Iro," spoke Poneiva. "I think you might return to your home now. Perhaps stay there a while and keep out of trouble, eh?"

The man was suddenly dejected. "I shall try, my Lord Poneiva." Obviously thinking of his marital situation.

"Ah, one more matter," spoke Bafa. "Did you ever meet the man Ruata, a noble who served Momana?"

"Oh, many times! And not just at Momana's house. Indeed, I saw him right here at least twice." He leaned forward and confided, "And I know he met with Ikataki."

That was exceedingly interesting. "We should learn if anyone else in this house knows Ruata," I said, as soon as Iro had scuttled out.

Bafa agreed. "And perhaps Lady Ma'ave could be of more use to us. She would be decidedly interested in Ikataki's possible involvement in this."

And would quite willingly cut his throat. Or at least ruin his political chances.

58. Of Marriages

The Lady Pua had come to escort her soon-to-be-unmarried daughter to her house. Having their combined wiles would be even better. As to Ruata, some knew the name but nothing of him. I would guess — and guess correctly, I am sure — that more had seen him but did not know the name.

I had little time for Toare those days, and he little for me. At last, he came and let me know that he and Ulani would be leaving, first to the House of Marareta, then — he was uncertain. "I think the master wants to stop at Isa's house," he said. "Perhaps we shall find our way to A'auwa later." He raised his eyes to me. "Before you or after you. But it will not be with you, will it, Teme?"

"No, my storytelling boy," I answered, and smiled. "Rahiniti will still be there for you to bother." And that was that, and he and Ulani walked away the next day. Not until after both had a good breakfast.

Pua and Ma'ave, mother and daughter, spoke privately with their High King a little later that day. Oh, very well, not privately for I was there too. "Ikataki?" asked Ma'ave. "Ah, trying to play both ends against each other and position himself to be High King."

Pua saw it. "He could blame the traditionalists if Poneiva were assassinated and ride the result to the High King's dais." She thought further. "And he might have encouraged those assassins."

"Not directly," I said. "He had Ruata for that. He had Momana. Who knows who else?" Bafa was not in attendance so I had to pretend to be him, that day. I think I did well. "And," I added, "he would just as soon Momana had been disgraced and I killed."

"Removing both you and giving him traditionalists to blame," finished Ma'ave. "It can't be proven, can it?"

Poneiva shook his head gravely. My brother did that well and looked wiser than he was. "No," I said, "but there is enough to ruin his reputation, maybe." I grinned my most wicked grin. Some say it the most wicked they have seen! "We might tell him this and hint we know more."

"He might just be willing to retire from politics," allowed Lady Pua.

Ma'ave agreed. "And if he doesn't, there is nothing to prevent three women from spreading rumors. There is enough evidence to make people believe what we say."

Poneiva only nodded, more gravely than before, and ordered beer.

Many wondered, in the months after, why Ikataki had suddenly retired to his house and no longer took part in politics. Then, they mostly forgot him.

I didn't. It was on his order I was almost murdered and, quite possibly, my brother too. But maybe being made nobody was worse punishment for Ikataki than being slain.

"So that would seem ended," said Bafa, when I told him the tale later. We sat together on my brother's back porch. That gave the best view of his gardens. Admittedly they were a bit withered, with the drier season on us. He should plant more citrus, I thought. That stays a dark green year round.

Once I had sat on porches with others, and that was good. But this was better. "So we should move on to other things," I told him. Perhaps I had lagged too long before my reply came, but my mind had been turning things over and looking under them.

"How about marriage?" he asked.

"Just what I had in mind, silly Bafa." I sighed. "I suppose we should tell my brothers."

"Indeed," he said. "Sooner or later."

59. Things Foretold

"We must prepare for a wedding in this house!" proclaimed Poneiva. "A great wedding! The gardens —"

"No," I said in a tone I hoped would allow no argument, "I shall bathe in the Pool of the Moon and Hito will be my protector and Taona Marareta will wed us by A'auwa. So it will be."

"I'll be there too," said Bafa.

"I should think so," was Beka's comment. "I suspected this was coming." He glanced toward our brother. "Poneiva had no clue, of course."

"It is true," Poneiva agreed. "When did this happen?"

Bafa laughed. "You all know Teme set her aim on me years ago. She rarely misses."

"But I thought her target had changed," said my brother, the High King. "So be it. By A'auwa you will wed and I shall be there."

I glanced at my husband-to-be. "I think we two can leave at once." And we did, not quite at once, but the next day, taking canoe down Teiri. With us traveled Oorto and Ruiru, and also Pua and Ma'ave, going to what was once the House of Temani'itu. Now the House of Naio was it named. Our own destination was Marareta's house first. We couldn't get married if we didn't tell the taona to come, could we?

It is to be admitted I did not want to leave that morning, leave my sleeping chamber in the House of the High King, where Bafa lay beside me. We had waited long, had we not? But when it was time, it was time, and I thank many gods that time came.

From Pua's home, where we stayed a night and departed from her and Ma'ave — though I invited both to the wedding — we paddled on to the Teoma and then the House of Marareta. Not unexpectedly, my brother's messengers had brought the taona the news before we could.

"We shall travel to A'auwa with you," promised Lady Mehetu. I was surprised to find her there, for I had left her with her new husband by the lake. "I came here after the death of Hoka." She paused a moment, in thought. "I think Hito and I shall continue to live such a life, sometimes together, sometimes apart. At least for some time."

Oorto went immediately to Marareta's son, grown a little older, a little taller, than when last I had seen him. Black of hair, as most Mora, but sea-eyed like his father, was Maratoa, and still reminded me of his birth mother, Pana'a, more than any other. "Will he come with us?" I asked. Oorto, too, looked to Marareta for an answer.

"Perhaps it is time Pana'a saw him again," said the taona, but did not quite sound certain of this. "You two will come?" he asked, looking to Oorto and Ruiru.

"Of course," stated my former bodyguard. "I could not miss Lady Teme's wedding."

Oorto looked back to the boy and the two stared at each other for a moment before the Diwarna slowly nodded his head. "Yes," he said. "Already he senses things others can not." He gave something of a crooked smile. "He reminds me of his mother." Oorto meant Rahaita, who adopted him.

242

The shaman carried on a quiet conversation with the little boy while the rest of us settled on the porch and conversed of a great many things, things done, things to be done. It was in the pidgin Oorto spoke, for he had never become particularly fluent in our Mora tongue. Maratoa seemed to follow him well enough, answering his friendly questions about nothing much.

"I should have expected you and Bafa to end up together," said the taona. "Not so long ago it seemed a sure thing. Then —"

"Then she went off to her brother's house and met Revaru," Bafa finished for him. "I thought it best not to chase after her. She was still a girl then."

"Almost did Mehetu's son win me while you dawdled and played with your stones," I informed him.

"I'll let you play with them too," he promised.

That might have been the best thing he had ever said to me. That and offering to teach me to shoot a bow, when I was only fifteen. What if I had not picked up that bow, not learned to launch an arrow and strike what I desired? All would be different. I thanked the god I had so recently chosen as my patron, Wenatu, and all the gods of the heavens.

We stayed a while in that house and then all traveled south. All — the taona's complete family, Mehetu, and we who had come to him. But again, I might have been willing to stay longer, walking the gardens with Bafa, sharing our chamber through the hot nights and sometimes rising then, too, to walk among Marareta's trees, the air thick with the scent of citrus blossoms.

But south we paddled on Teoma, in several canoes, the way not so hard now in a season of lower water. Up from the first falls we walked, up past the Pool of the Moon where I soon would bathe, and beheld A'auwa. "So," spoke Oorto. "It is as beautiful as you say, Mika." That was how he named Marareta, the name the Diwarna had given him. "Even more beautiful than the lakes beyond the mountains." I didn't know how anyone could have doubted it.

It was growing late; the children were tired of walking, and we were tired of walking and sometimes carrying them. But the House of Arierona lay near, and the torches were being lit beside the lake. And there stood Pana'a, awaiting us.

She looked at little Maratoa, tenderly, a bit sadly, before speaking — to me. "I said, before you left, that there might be more to the prophecy of those who came from the sea. Now I see this. Your son will be raised to the dais of the High King and so once more is fulfilled the promise that the Hero from the Sea will give all the land its king."

Then she spoke a prophecy as do they who dwell on the Sacred Isle.

In fullness does the Hero now
give to all the land its king.
At the Sacred Lake are wed
they who will complete the tale.

We went into the House of Arierona to greet the king and rest.

244

60. The Bow of Wenatu

"So, I let you go away with Bafa and you steal him from me?" asked Rahiniti.

"You should have known better. I can steal any woman's man!" She giggled quite a long time at that. I didn't really think I was that funny. "Will you come with me to the Pool of the Moon?"

"Of course, Teme. Ah, you are marrying!" She began crying and seized onto me. "I will miss you even more now!"

"You know you can stay in this house. Or the High King's or wherever. You can live with me and Bafa." I considered that. "But don't expect to be a second wife!" That started her giggling again.

But she sobered fairly quickly. "I could be Hito's second wife, maybe. We still like each other. Maybe more than that even. But it might not be so good for either of us."

I could only agree with that. But what did I know? "Demba invited you to come and stay with her and Gordie as long as you want. Maybe you would like that."

"Maybe. But the House of Gordie is in the middle of nothing!"

Not so much anymore. I would not get into all that right now. I could give her my complete story some other time.

"My brothers and Aranu and all their families are on the way," I told her. Arierona had informed me just that morning that a messenger had come. "We will plan the wedding for three days after their arrival." That would give everyone time to go through any rituals, for Bafa to follow the proper taboos, for the feast to be readied!

Toare and Ulani had already shown up. "I shall compose the epic of your journey, Lady Teme," Ulani had informed me. "I don't trust Toare with it. It is a little too personal for him." He gave me a smile and a bit of a wink. "But he has come up with some number of sad songs recently!"

"Ha, maybe he and Marareta could be Kohari minstrels, playing on the sef and warbling sentimental songs!" The taona did love to strum the three strings of the Kohari instrument he had procured and sing songs of his homeland in an odd soft and low voice. Everyone knows singing should be high and clear so one may follow the stories.

"I shall give them that recommendation." He sat for a short while, without speaking, and we watched others walk by us on the porch. "Oorto is here, I know. He has a lover?"

"Yes, Master Ulani. It is so — the warrior Ruiru. Hmm, or priest Ruiru now, I think."

"That is good," he said and never spoke more of it.

Then came all those from the House of the High King and things hurtled forward. Came, too, Lady Pua — but not Ma'ave — and my father and mother, and then, a great surprise, King Ruapata of the kingdom just north of Areirona's, and his young wife, Va'ai. They had come to the marriage of Rahaita and Marareta, I remembered, and counted themselves their friends. I was honored that they would count me so too. Both had shown valor during the war, when Hara'a invaded their land.

And the eve of my wedding, at last. How had it come so soon? Bafa would be in a sweat lodge somewhere this evening, after fasting through the day and I — ah, I would at last bathe beneath Pana'a, in the Pool of the Moon, and ask the blessing of Marahina on my marriage. Many children? Well, some! And Pana'a had already promised one, hadn't she?

He would be very handsome like his father and brave like his mother! With Hito as my protector, Rahiniti as my companion, I walked along the path by A'auwa in the late afternoon. There had been a light rain earlier and now the sun broke through, with all its promises.

Above A'auwa stood a rainbow, Wenatu's great curved bow and I, Teme, had been struck by his arrows of heaven. Good aim had Wenatu!

Ulani had spoken truly. One story's end was another's start. Tomorrow, Bafa and I would stand, clothed in white, crowned with feathers, before the Taona Marareta and begin a new story.

And tonight I washed away the dust of the last one, the road I had traveled, away and back.

Afterword

"Arrows of Heaven" is the second Mora novel, following "God of Rain" and continuing the saga begun in the three Malvern books. A third novel, telling of Rahiniti, will complete the Mora trilogy.

A note about pronunciations of Mora names: typically, all the vowels in these are pronounced separately, even when we have a string of them in a row. Thus Mouiri is spoken MOE-oo-EER-ee. I have used an apostrophe to indicate the stop between repeated vowel sounds, as in A'auwa, pronounced AH-ah-OO-wah.

As for words from the Kohari language, I leave you to make your best guess.

Author and artist Stephen Brooke lives and works in an old farmhouse in the Florida Panhandle. All his books are available from Arachis Press, a small publisher dedicated to presenting meaningful literature for readers of all ages.

Visit http://arachispress.com for our catalog.

www.ingramcontent.com/pod-product-compliance
Lightning Source LLC
Chambersburg PA
CBHW060351030726
47497CB00003B/671